DANGER FROM ABOVE!

The stone fell with surprising slowness. Meat imagined that this was because his heart had sped up a thousand times. He'd read about this. A person's whole life really could pass before his eyes when the heart sped up a thousand times.

The limbs of the trees around him were moved by a sudden gust of wind. Leaves rustled, branches cracked. The wind was so sudden it seemed unearthly, like the woman in the tower.

If the stone tried to go this way or that way, the wind would correct it and send it . . . to him!

Then the stone seemed to flutter as if it had suddenly sprouted wings. That would not have surprised Meat. Nothing would ever surprise him again. Wind, wings, whatever—that stone was going where it was intended to go.

Whoever had thrown the stone was shouting something, but Meat couldn't make it out.

A cry cut through the late afternoon air, drowning out all other sound.

Meat knew that cry even though he had never heard anything like it before. It was the cry of someone about to die.

And it had come from his throat.

A HERCULEAH JONES MYSTERY

THE BLACK TOWER

BY BETSY BYARS

SLEUTH
PUFFIN

PUFFIN BOOKS

Published by the Penguin Group

Penguin Group (USA) Inc., 345 Hudson Street, New York, New York 10014, U.S.A.

Penguin Group (Canada), 90 Eglinton Avenue East, Suite 700, Toronto, Ontario, Canada M4P 2Y3
(a division of Pearson Penguin Canada Inc.)

Penguin Books Ltd, 80 Strand, London WC2R 0RL, England

Penguin Ireland, 25 St Stephen's Green, Dublin 2, Ireland (a division of Penguin Books Ltd)

Penguin Group (Australia), 250 Camberwell Road, Camberwell, Victoria 3124, Australia
(a division of Pearson Australia Group Pty Ltd)

Penguin Books India Pvt Ltd, 11 Community Centre, Panchsheel Park, New Delhi - 110 017, India

Penguin Group (NZ), 67 Apollo Drive, Rosedale, North Shore 0745, Auckland, New Zealand
(a division of Pearson New Zealand Ltd.)

Penguin Books (South Africa) (Pty) Ltd, 24 Sturdee Avenue,
Rosebank, Johannesburg 2196, South Africa

Registered Offices: Penguin Books Ltd, 80 Strand, London WC2R 0RL, England

First published in the United States of America by Viking,
a division of Penguin Young Readers Group, 2006
This Sleuth edition published by Puffin Books, a division of Penguin Young Readers Group, 2007

5 7 9 10 8 6 4

THE LIBRARY OF CONGRESS HAS CATALOGED THE VIKING EDITION AS FOLLOWS:

Byars, Betsy Cromer.
The black tower / by Betsy Byars.
p.   cm.—(A Herculeah Jones mystery)
Summary: Herculeah Jones gets involved in another dangerous mystery when she
goes to visit old Mr. Shivers Hunt, resident of the forbidding Hunt House.
ISBN 0-670-06174-3 (hardcover)
[1. Mystery and detective stories.] I. Title.
PZ7.B9836Bit 2006   [Fic]—dc22   2005033317

Puffin Books ISBN 978-0-14-240937-4

Printed in the United States of America

Set in Minion
Book design by Sam Kim

CONTENTS

A HERCULEAH JONES MYSTERY

THE BLACK TOWER

THE TERROR IN BLACK TOWER

Slowly she climbed the circular stairs in the tower, drawn against her will to what waited at the top.

Halfway there, she paused. She heard the sound of the tower door close below her. Had it been a hand that closed it? She looked down. The thought that she might be trapped made her dizzy.

She touched the wall to steady herself. There was an eerie coldness to the stones beneath her hand.

She lifted her head. She listened.

She heard nothing, but she knew someone was up there, waiting for her.

And whoever it was knew she was coming.

Slowly she took another step and another. Higher . . . higher. With each step, her fear grew until it seemed to swirl around her like a cape that held no warmth.

Herculeah stopped reading and let the book fall to her lap. "Are you positive this is the book you want me to read?" she asked.

The old man on the bed blinked his eyes once. That meant "yes."

"Well, I'm getting spooked," Herculeah said. "Particularly because this house, your house, has a tower attached to it. It's exactly like this one, isn't it?"

One blink. Yes.

"Have you ever been up there?"

Yes.

"What's up there? Oh, I forgot. You can't answer that kind of question. Only yes or no. Is there a room up there?"

Yes.

"Does the tower have circular stairs?"

Yes.

"That was stupid of me. I guess all towers do. Either that or they have a ladder."

Herculeah glanced out the window. She could see the tower now. It rose, black and forbidding, part of the house and yet somehow separate. Halfway up the tower there were windows. They were slits so deep in the stone that no daylight could come through.

Herculeah paused in thought. Her hands tightened on the book in her lap. The silence continued.

Herculeah had come here to read to Mr. Hunt. Her mother,

a private detective, had asked her to do this. Mr. Hunt was, or had been, one of her mother's clients.

"Why was he a client?" Herculeah had asked, instantly curious. "What did he want you to do?"

"That doesn't concern you."

Herculeah had leaned forward, more interested than ever. "What did he want you to find? That's what all old people want you to do—find someone or something from their past."

Her mother's wry smile made Herculeah think she had hit the mark.

"So what could it have been?" she went on thoughtfully. "What could have happened? Murder? Was it a murder?" Her gray eyes lit up. "It was murder, wasn't it?"

"Whatever it was happened a long time ago."

"So it was murder."

Her mother lifted one hand to silence her. "If you're going to play detective—"

"Mom, I don't *play* detective. I have solved six murders." She began to count them on her fingers. "Mr. Crewell, Madame Rosa . . ."

Her mom sighed, and Herculeah discontinued her list. "Oh, all right, what do you want me to do?"

"Just read to him for an hour or so. The man is lonely. He can't move at all since his stroke. He can only blink his eyes— one blink for yes, two for no."

"How awful! Sure, I'll do it. Actually, I enjoy reading to

people. What kind of book would an old man like? Something about old horses, old airplanes, or"—she grinned—"old women? I'll take a bunch of books so he'll have a choice. First thing tomorrow I'll go to the library and load up with books."

"Oh, there's a huge library at the house. You won't need to take anything."

"A huge library? This old man has a huge library in his house?"

Her mom hesitated a moment before she answered. "Have you ever heard of Shivers Hunt?"

"Mom! Not *the* Shivers Hunt!"

"There couldn't be but one."

"Mom, you mean I'd actually get to go inside Haunt House?"

"What?"

"Haunt House. That's what all the kids call it. And, Mom, nobody has ever been inside it. I cannot believe that I'm going to Haunt House."

"Well, you aren't going unless you stop calling it that."

"Right! Hunt House!"

"I won't let you go unless you promise you won't do anything to upset Mr. Hunt."

"I won't, I won't! I promise! But I can't help being excited. I, Herculeah Jones, am going inside"—she swallowed the word—"Hunt House."

But when Herculeah got there, she hadn't been taken to the

library to choose a book as she had expected. The nurse took her straight up the stairs to Mr. Hunt's bedroom. The book had already been chosen for her. It was waiting on the table by the old man's bed.

Herculeah picked up the book. She read the title aloud. "*The Terror in Black Tower*. This is what I'm supposed to read?" she asked the nurse.

"Yes, Herculeah. When I told Mr. Hunt that you were coming to read to him, I asked if there was any particular book he'd like. He blinked yes. I must have carried a hundred books up from the library before he finally saw this one and gave a very definite yes."

Herculeah picked up the book. On the cover, embossed in the black leather, was the silhouette of a tower. It was outlined in gold, but it looked as if someone had rubbed their fingers over the gold, as if to erase the whole tower from sight. It gave the book a sinister look. She rubbed her own fingers over the gold, then stopped abruptly.

"Well, let's get on with it." She opened the book. "Ready, Mr. Hunt?"

Yes.

Inside, the pages were thick and yellow with age. They smelled of mildew and dark passages and old secrets. Herculeah loved it.

Perhaps, she thought, Mr. Hunt had read the book as a boy,

and back then it had seemed scary, probably full of family madness and secret passages, and—who knows?—maybe some terror actually had been up in the black tower.

But those things didn't exist in modern times.

They didn't.

She paused.

Or did they?

THE TRAPDOOR

Herculeah glanced at Mr. Hunt. He was waiting for her to continue. She looked down at the page.

"Where was I? Oh, yes, she's going up the tower steps." Herculeah smiled. "Actually, this will probably sound foolish to you, Mr. Hunt, but I can understand the girl doing this. I mean, she knows she's not supposed to. She knows there's something up there, something dangerous. But she can't stop herself. That's the way I am. I would do the exact same thing. The only difference would be that at this point my hair would be frizzling. I have radar hair. It gets bigger when I'm in danger. Like this."

She laughed and fluffed out her hair. Mr. Hunt watched. His bright bird eyes never left her face.

At that moment, her hair actually seemed to be frizzling on its own, as if it were anticipating the day she would climb the tower, the day she—heart racing with fear—not the character in the book, would take those circular stairs.

She patted her hair into place and said, "Oh, here's where we were." She began to read.

Slowly she took another step and another. Higher . . . higher. With each step, her fear grew until it seemed to swirl around her like a cape that held no warmth.

In the distance came the sound of thunder. She glanced out the window. She could see nothing through the dense, chilling fog that circled the tower.

A storm was coming. She must hurry.

Still she hesitated before taking the next step. Only eight steps remained. She could see the heavy wooden door at the top now, a trapdoor.

Only seven steps.

Now she could hear it. The sound of breathing seemed to move from side to side behind the trapdoor. It was as if whoever, whatever was there, was trying to find a way out.

"I'm coming," she whispered.

The door to the bedroom opened behind Herculeah, and, startled, she spun around.

"Your hour's up, Herculeah," the nurse said.

"Already? I just started. I've hardly read two pages. I got

started talking about myself—I do that all the time. Plus I was getting to the good part. The girl in the book was hearing breathing. I've got to find out what's doing that breathing."

"Sorry. It'll keep. Tomorrow the print will still be right there waiting for you."

"I know." Herculeah sighed. "Actually I read a lot of books, and I've learned that authors save important things—things like what's waiting up in the tower, doing that heavy breathing—until the very end. If I know authors, this one will start a flashback just when she gets to the trapdoor. Then, on the last page—finally, finally—we'll find out what was in the tower."

"You must do a lot of reading."

"Yes."

"But we don't want to tire Mr. Hunt."

"No. Did I tire you, Mr. Hunt?"

Two blinks. No.

"But did I scare you?"

No.

She laughed. "Well, I scared myself."

Herculeah folded a ribbon into the book to hold her place. She closed the book and set it on the table.

"I'll be back tomorrow to pick up. Remember where we left off? It's getting ready to storm. The girl heard thunder. It'll be a dark and stormy night when anything can happen." She gave her words a dramatic reading.

He blinked a forceful yes.

"Dramatic things always happen during storms—though it's dramatic enough with something waiting for her at the top of the tower."

Another forceful yes.

"Do you know what's up there?"

Yes.

"Because you've read the book before?"

"Time," the nurse reminded her.

"I have to go." Herculeah smiled at the old man, his face pale against the pillows, his bright bird eyes trying to tell her something, something important.

The nurse said, "Your friend is waiting for you outside."

"Meat?"

"I think that's his name. I tried to get him to come inside, but he wouldn't."

"That's Meat."

Herculeah almost explained that Meat was afraid of this house, that he half believed the ghost stories that surrounded it, believed the stories that the portraits had holes in the eyes so that someone in a secret passage behind the wall could watch your every move.

"Meat . . . Herculeah . . ." the nurse said. "What wonderful names!"

"Meat got his because there's a lot of him. I got mine because my mom was watching a Hercules movie when she was waiting for me to be born. Mom was kidding around about naming me

Hercules if I was a boy. The nurse said, 'What about if it's a girl?' Mom said, 'She'll be Herculeah.' I guess I was lucky. The doctor got in the act and said, 'How about Samson?' He even sang it, 'Oh, Samson-ya!'" She laughed. "Anyway, everyone who knows me says it suits."

"I only met you this afternoon," the nurse said, "but I think it suits you, too."

As they moved into the hall, Herculeah said, "You know, I can't stop wondering why he chose this book." She smiled. "Although I'm always looking for the reasons people do things."

"I wondered about that, too."

"Really?"

"Because I've had other patients like Mr. Hunt, patients who have been deprived of everything but their minds. And it seems that another sense has been heightened. They seem to know what's ahead, the way an animal can sense a storm."

"Premonitions."

"Yes. If Mr. Hunt had some way of knowing there would be trouble in that tower, he would have picked this book. Well, I've got to get back to my patient."

"Right. I'll see you both tomorrow."

"Oh, I won't be here," the nurse said, smiling. "New grand-child. A Miss Wegman is taking over for me. Do you need me to show you the way out?"

"No, I remember the way."

"Because this house has a lot of halls that don't go anywhere and oddly shaped rooms. It's easy to get lost in here."

"I won't."

She started down the stairs. She was lost in thought until she glanced at the painting on the wall. It was a family portrait: old man Hunt—Lionus Hunt, who had built the house—his wife, and the four children. Mr. Shivers Hunt was the oldest of the children. Then there was a younger sister and twin girls.

Herculeah paused, half hoping to see someone peering at her through holes in the old man's eyes.

Oh, well, she told herself, it was too much to hope for.

She was turning to go when something about the twins caught her eye. The twins were dressed alike—in middy blouses—but there was something about the blouse of the smaller twin.

She bent closer. She rubbed her fingers over the painting. The figure of the smaller twin had been damaged in some way. It had been repaired, but not by the same artist who had done the original picture. Strange.

Strange, too, about Mr. Hunt's choosing the book. There was so much she didn't know, so much she would have to find out.

With a shiver of anticipation, she continued down the stairs.

3

HAUNT HOUSE

"I thought you were never coming out," Meat said. He got up from the steps and brushed off the back of his jeans.

Herculeah glanced at her watch. "Five o'clock. Right on time."

"I thought something had happened to you," he confessed. "I thought you were never coming out."

"Oh, Meat, that's silly. Just because you thought you saw me get stabbed that one time, now you think you have to protect me."

"It's the kind of house where things like that happen," he explained. "A person goes in and they never come out."

"You've listened to too many ghost stories."

"I have never trusted a house that has—well . . . that has a face," he finished in a rush.

"A face?"

"Yeah. That huge door is the mouth, and those windows seem to be eyes looking at us."

"You know what this reminds me of? The time we went to the amusement park and you wouldn't go in the funhouse because the front was like a clown face, and you were afraid to walk in his mouth."

"I was not afraid. I just prefer doors that look like doors." He decided to change the subject. "So, tell me everything."

"Well," Herculeah said, "first the nurse and I walked upstairs, and, Meat"—she lowered her voice—"eyes watched me from a portrait every step of the way."

"Get outta here," Meat said. He was proud that he hadn't sounded as if he believed her, but then he spoiled it by adding, "They didn't really, did they?"

"No, they didn't."

Meat said, "Let's go."

"What's your hurry?"

He glanced up at the house. With the sun setting behind it, the house cast deep shadows over the ground. A dense area of woods circled the house and seemed to be reaching for whoever was unfortunate enough to step off the drive.

Meat's first impression of the place had made him shudder. If he had not been with Herculeah, he would have turned and run for his life, but she had been beside him, giving him the history of the house.

"It was built over a hundred years ago by old Mr. Hunt, Lionus Hunt. See, Meat, Lionus Hunt had been like a field hand on this big estate in England, and when he got over here and struck it rich, he built the exact same house, only he'd never been inside the house so he had to make up the rooms. They're all crazy."

Meat didn't doubt that.

"And from the first day, Meat, the house was struck by tragedy."

Meat didn't doubt that, either.

As Meat had gotten closer, he had seen the tower. He had known there would be one. Herculeah had told him that and had said, "Guess what it's called."

"I can't."

"Shivers Tower."

Well, it made him shiver, all right.

"But the tower's been locked up," she had said, "because there was some terrible tragedy there. My mom claims she doesn't know what the tragedy was, but I'm going to find out. And, Meat, there's supposed to be money hidden somewhere in the house. Old man Hunt didn't trust banks so all the millions and millions are in the walls or the secret room or the tower."

"Can we change the subject?" Meat asked.

"Yes, but guess what happened today?" Herculeah said as they started for home down the long drive.

"What?"

"When I was reading to Mr. Hunt—"

Something cold seemed to touch Meat's neck, and he glanced over his shoulder. He gasped with fright.

In one of the upstairs windows, a face was framed, a face in a tangle of wild hair. The eyes stared down at him with a look of such wildness that it froze his blood.

He stopped. He couldn't move. He closed his eyes.

"What's wrong?" Herculeah asked. She had continued on a few steps and now turned to look at him.

"A face," he managed to say.

"What face?"

"In the window."

As he spoke, he saw the face again in his mind, and he felt the image was there permanently, the way looking at the sun can leave the eye scarred with the image.

"Which window?"

He pointed a trembling finger.

Herculeah shaded her eyes from the setting sun. "I don't see anything."

He forced himself to look. Of course there was nothing there now.

"It was a face—I don't know how to describe it—an evil face. There was a lot of wild hair—"

"Like mine?" she asked, grinning and fluffing her hair.

Herculeah wouldn't be serious. "No. No! This was hair that hadn't been combed in years—maybe never—and the face, well, it was like, like a bird of prey, and I was the prey. And the fingers were like talons and—"

"You saw the hands, too?"

"No, but those were the kind of terrible hands that would go with the face. . . ."

Herculeah smiled.

"It really isn't amusing," Meat said.

"I know. I was smiling at myself. It's just that this is the kind of house that makes you think you see things, makes you think you hear things. When I was reading about the girl going up the tower steps, I actually imaged I was the girl and—"

"This wasn't my imagination."

"All right." She looked thoughtful. "I think Mr. Hunt does have a couple of sisters. I don't even know if one of them lives in this house, but if she does, maybe that was who you saw."

"*What* I saw is more like it. That face might not even have been human."

She looked at him closely. His face was as pale as if he had seen a ghost.

"Let's go home."

"Gladly."

They walked through the open gates. On either gate, the figure of a lion was worked into the wrought iron. One paw was raised as if, Meat thought, to menace visitors as they passed through.

"And the owner, Lionus Hunt," Herculeah said, speaking as if she were reading from a guide book, "had these gates made in his likeness to guard the house. He wanted visitors to know the house was his and that they entered at their own peril."

"Did you read that somewhere?"

"No, I just made it up."

"Well, if he really wanted to menace people," Meat said, "he could have used that old woman's face."

MAN OR BEAST

"Let me," Meat said, reaching for the doorbell. Over his shoulder he said, "I hate this doorbell. It's like the ding-dong of doom."

It was the next day, and Meat had walked Herculeah to Hunt House for her second reading of *The Terror in Black Tower*.

It was one of those old-timey doorbells that had to be turned, and Meat gave it a manly twist. From deep within the house came the ding-dong.

They heard heavy footsteps. "It's a new nurse today," Herculeah said. "I think her name's Miss—"

The door opened then, stopping Herculeah's sentence. Herculeah and Meat looked up. The smiles on their faces faded.

Nurse Wegman was big. Meat had seen bodies like that on *World Class Wrestling*. She was not as big as his father, of course. Few people were. After all, his dad was Macho Man, a championship wrestler. Just the thought of his dad brought back the picture of him entering the ring, the crowd chanting, "Macho,

Macho, Macho Man." He could hear the music, feel the pride, the—

Meat's pleasant picture was shattered by one harsh word from the nurse. "Yes?"

"I'm Herculeah Jones."

Nurse Wegman said another word. "So?"

"Didn't anybody tell you? I read to Mr. Hunt every afternoon at four o'clock. It's four now." She lifted her arm to display her watch.

Meat thought Nurse Wegman looked as if she didn't trust Herculeah, so he came immediately to his friend's defense. "It's all right, Nurse. Her mom's a private investigator. She works for Mr. Hunt."

That seemed to help Nurse Wegman make up her mind. "You'd better come in."

Herculeah went inside, and Meat said, "I'll wait out here in case you need me."

"You aren't coming in?" Nurse Wegman asked.

"No, sir."

Meat turned away quickly, his face red with embarrassment. He hoped neither Miss Wegman nor Herculeah had heard that "sir."

Inside, Herculeah followed Nurse Wegman up the stairs. "Your mother is a private detective?" the nurse asked.

"Yes."

"What, exactly, is she investigating?"

"I don't know. She doesn't confide in me."

"I was only asking because I've heard rumors about this place. People seem to think it's kind of spooky." Her voice seemed to deepen. "I've even heard there's money hidden in here. Have you heard that?"

"Yes, I heard the Hunts didn't believe in banks."

"Are there any rumors where it might be hidden?"

"Not that I've heard. It could be anywhere."

"And this is a big house."

"Yes." Herculeah watched Miss Wegman's broad back, the ponytail that swung between her shoulder blades. At least, she thought, this nurse was big enough to take care of an invalid. "The book I'm reading to Mr. Hunt is *The Terror in Black Tower*, and this house even has a black tower, in case you didn't notice."

"I noticed."

Nurse Wegman opened the door to Mr. Hunt's bedroom. "I'll be around if you need me."

Herculeah approached the bed. "Hi," she told Mr. Hunt, "it's me again—Herculeah. Do you feel like hearing some more about the girl in the tower?"

For a moment Mr. Hunt didn't seem to recognize her. His eyes weren't as bright as yesterday.

"Do you want me to read?"

Three blinks.

What did that mean? Herculeah wondered. One blink meant "yes"; two meant "no." Three meant what?

"Are you trying to tell me something, Mr. Hunt?"

One blink. Yes.

"Is it about the book?"

No.

She had a sudden insight and she asked, "Is it about Nurse Wegman?"

Yes.

"Is she—?"

From the doorway Nurse Wegman said, "If you came to read, read!" It was a command.

"I'd better read," Herculeah said. "Don't you think?"

Yes.

"And I'll be sitting right out here to make sure everything's"—Nurse Wegman paused as if trying to find the right words—"all right."

Herculeah picked up the book, opened it, and glanced down at the page.

"Ah, yes," she said. Herculeah was smiling, but there was a false cheer in her voice. "The girl is still on the stairs. You know, people have climbed Everest in the time it's taken this girl to get to the top of the tower."

Although the man on the bed could not move or speak, he seemed on occasion to send off signals—brain waves, maybe. At any rate, sometimes Herculeah seemed to know what he was thinking. Maybe, as the nurse suggested yesterday, Mr. Hunt had developed special powers.

"Yes," she agreed, "that's true. People want to get to the top of Everest, and this girl definitely does not want to get to the top of the tower." She lifted the book to the light. "But I do admit I wish she'd hurry up." She began to read.

She took two more steps. The noise above her was unlike anything she had heard before. It was not a human sound, and it was not the sound of an animal—at least not any animal she had ever heard before.

Herculeah glanced up at the man on the bed. She grinned. "Man or beast?" she asked, trying to turn his attention to the book.

And the silent answer that seemed to come from the man on the bed was, "Beast."

A PREMONITION

"You're awfully quiet," Meat said.

He and Herculeah had left the grounds of Hunt House and were entering their own neighborhood. Now, in familiar surroundings, seeing familiar signs—BERNIE HOLDEN: ACCOUNTANT, BESSIE FLOWER: ALTERATIONS, CAKES BY CHERI, ONE-DAY DENTURES—Meat felt he was capable of holding an intelligent conversation.

"I'm thinking," she said.

"About the book? Is it getting better?"

"The book couldn't get any better. It started strong and scary. That's my kind of book."

Meat glanced at her quickly. "But why would you choose a book like that to read to someone who's sick?"

"I didn't have any choice."

"You always have a choice."

"Not this time. The book was chosen for me. Mr. Hunt picked it out himself."

"How could he? I thought he could only blink."

"The nurse—this was the other nurse, the one I liked, not Nurse Wegman—brought in hundreds of books, and he blinked at this one."

"I wonder why."

"Who knows. I tried to figure it out. It could be that he read the book a long time ago when he was a boy. And—this just occurred to me—in the book, there's somebody up in the tower, a prisoner maybe, and since Mr. Hunt probably feels like a prisoner himself . . . he's identifying with the prisoner."

"Yes, but you'd think, if he does feel like a prisoner, he'd want to hear a story about people outside doing things—climbing mountains and forging streams, looking for buried treasure."

"Or maybe," she said thoughtfully, "he's trying to warn us about the tower. The nurse said she'd had patients in Mr. Hunt's condition who got premonitions about the future. I hope that's not the case, because something terrible is going to happen and—"

She broke off and lifted her head. "That's strange," she said.

They were now at the front steps of Herculeah's house. Her face was lifted to the window.

"What?"

"The phone."

"What about it?"

"It's ringing."

"What's strange about that?" Meat asked. "That's what phones do."

Herculeah's face had that serious look, so he changed his question. "Why do you think it's strange?"

"Look at my hair."

"It's frizzling," he said.

"Yes! Exactly! As soon as I heard the phone ringing, my hair started doing this."

"The phone's stopped ringing now," Meat said. "Your hair can go back to normal."

Herculeah didn't answer. It was as if she were listening to something happening inside the house. Meat didn't hear a thing.

"Your mom probably answered," he said.

"Mom's not home."

"Then someone's leaving a message."

"That's what I'm thinking. The message is for me."

"You don't know that."

Herculeah reached for the banister and started quickly up the steps.

Meat followed. "This is what I don't get," he said to her back. "Your hair is frizzling, which means there's danger, and here you are hurrying into the house. If there's danger, why would you go to meet it?"

She turned and looked at him. Her gray eyes were dark with concern. "Because I might not be the one in danger. Someone may need me."

She unlocked the door and went inside, leaving Meat alone on the steps.

Well, *he* wasn't going inside. He'd never been foolish enough to rush to meet danger. Anyway, he knew Herculeah would tell him about it. She was very generous about sharing her danger.

He glanced across the street at his house. He could go home, but there wouldn't be anything to do there. He sat down on the steps.

Inside, Herculeah stood in the hallway for a moment. She listened. Someone was leaving a message on her mother's office answering machine.

The voice was old and shaky, but Herculeah could make out the message. Her blood froze.

"Meat!"

There was such urgency in her voice that Meat couldn't help himself. He jumped up and went to meet the danger, too.

When he entered the living room, he saw that Herculeah was standing by her mother's desk. She was bending over the answering machine. "You have to hear this," she said.

Meat had the childish urge to put his fingers in his ears, but he resisted.

"Something's wrong, isn't it?"

"Yes."

"Is it very wrong, medium wrong or"—he paused hopefully—"just some little thing?" He had asked Herculeah this question before, and he knew how she would answer. "It's very wrong, isn't it?"

"Dead wrong."

THE WARNING

Meat moved closer to the desk.

"Listen," Herculeah said. With quick, practiced motions, she rewound the message and played it. An old shaky voice came from the machine.

"—s a murderer. Stay away from the—"

"You must not have rewound it all the way. Try it again."

She rewound the tape and replayed it.

Again the old voice said, "—s a murderer. Stay away from the—"

Well, Meat thought, maybe he couldn't begin the message for the old caller, but he sure could end it.

In the silence that followed, he finished the sentence. "Tower."

For emphasis, to make sure Herculeah got the message, he said, "Stay away from the tower."

"I hate it when people do that," Herculeah said.

"Do what?" Meat asked. "Leave warning messages on the answering machine?"

"No, I hate it when they start their warning message before waiting for the beep. Half the message is lost."

"I can finish the last half," Meat said. "It's—"

"I heard you before. I'm going to play it again."

"Good idea," Meat said. Listening to the message had obviously become an instant addiction with Herculeah. He wouldn't mind hearing it again himself.

"Listen real carefully this time. In the beginning of the message, I think the person was saying either 'He's a murderer' or 'She's a murderer.'"

"That's all there are—'he's' and 'she's.'"

"But they could have said a specific name."

"Either way, it didn't sound good to me."

She rewound the tape. "Listen."

"—s a murderer. Stay away from the—"

Meat couldn't help himself. He said, "Tower."

Herculeah glanced at him with irritation. "You don't know that it was tower."

"Then why do I keep hearing it in my mind? You hear things in your mind and believe them completely."

"You just think it's 'tower' because you're afraid of towers."

"I am not afraid of towers. I just can't see any good reason for putting one on a house. Oh, maybe if you had a mad relative that you wanted to keep out of sight—a tower would be good for that. Or if a parent had bad kids. I mean, 'Go to your room,' is nothing compared to, 'Go to the tower.'"

Herculeah didn't seem that interested. She plopped down in her mother's chair. "I think it was a woman's voice, don't you? Give me your thoughts."

"My only thought," he said, "is that it *is* a warning. I think that you should never go back to that house again."

Herculeah frowned. That was obviously not what she wanted to hear. "Anyway," she said with a shrug, "we can't be sure the message is for me."

"It's for you."

"It could be a wrong number."

"It's no wrong number."

"It could be for my mom. And my mom has lots of cases she's working on. It could be a warning to her."

"Yeah, right."

Herculeah leaned back in her mother's chair. Her mother, Mim Jones, used this front room for her office. She saw her clients here. And Herculeah, sitting in her mother's chair, always felt more like a detective than she usually did.

"I wonder," she said, picking up a pencil and putting it behind her ear as her mother sometimes did, "if I should let my mom hear this."

"Of course."

"I don't know. She might take it seriously."

"I should hope so."

"And make me stop going."

"You *should* stop going. Remember your hair frizzling. And your hair is never wrong."

"I can't stop. Things are just starting to get interesting. Let's listen one more time, and this time try to see if there's any background noise—any clocks ticking or doorbells ringing or cars in the street outside."

She rewound the machine and the message came again.

"—s a murderer. Stay away from the—"

Meat clamped his lips together so he couldn't say "tower," but it was not necessary. A voice spoke from the doorway.

"What's going on here?"

Herculeah and Meat looked up to see Herculeah's mother.

"What is going on here?" she repeated, separating the words to show her displeasure.

"Nothing," Meat stammered, but he knew it was not going to satisfy her. It wouldn't have satisfied her daughter. He then said something that might satisfy them all.

He said, "I'd better be getting home."

7

SOME SILLY IDEA

Meat crossed the room quickly only to find that Herculeah's mother, looking very immovable, was blocking the doorway.

"Excuse me," he said.

She didn't even do him the courtesy of looking at him. He cleared his throat, but that didn't do any good, either.

"What's going on, Herculeah? I want an answer. Now."

"Mom, nothing's going on," Herculeah said.

Good start, Meat thought.

"Anyway, it's not what you're thinking," Herculeah continued.

"You have no idea what I'm thinking."

Meat thought he knew. He remembered the last time Herculeah's mother had caught them in her office. They had been listening to one of her private taped conversations with the Moloch, and he was sure that was going through her mind as well as his own.

"We weren't snooping this time," he said, hoping to ease the situation. He wished he hadn't said "this time," because if she hadn't been thinking about that, then she would be now.

"I'll handle it, Meat," Herculeah said.

"Thanks."

Herculeah took a deep breath and lifted her head. This caused the pencil behind her ear to fall onto the desk. She carefully put it beside the yellow legal pad where she found it.

"When Meat and I came in the front door, we heard someone leaving a message. I thought it might be important, so we came in here to listen. That's the entire story. You're too suspicious."

"Was the message for me?"

"We don't know. It was anonymous."

"I'd better be going," Meat said.

Herculeah said, "Well, it wasn't so much anonymous. It was just a piece of a message, Mom. *Whoever left it* started too soon and broke off in the middle. It was an old person, and some old people aren't used to using answering machines."

"Old people are impatient, too, and sometimes won't wait for the beep, or they might not even know what a beep is," Meat offered, though he could see at once that no one was interested in his knowledge of old people.

"Play it," Herculeah's mom said.

"I've already heard it, so I'll be going."

This time it worked, and Herculeah's mom stepped aside, allowing him to move through the doorway.

As soon as the front door closed behind him, he felt instant relief, but almost immediately he wished he were back inside. He could be hearing what Herculeah and her mom were saying. If only he had been slower opening the door.

What Herculeah was saying was, "Listen for yourself."

The message was played, and in the silence that followed, Herculeah said, "Meat has some silly idea that the message was to warn us to stay away from the tower at Haunt—I mean, Hunt—House."

"I had a silly idea, too."

"Oh, Mom, you never have silly ideas."

She kept her eyes on her daughter. "My silly idea was that I could trust you to read to Mr. Hunt without stirring up trouble."

RETURN TO HAUNT HOUSE

"I can't believe your mom is letting you go back to read to Mr. Hunt," Meat said.

Herculeah didn't answer.

It was three thirty in the afternoon, and Meat and Herculeah were on their way to Hunt House.

They had been walking in silence. Herculeah had been admiring the fall afternoon, the way the leaves fell from the old trees. Meat was trying not to sound like his mother, though his last statement—"I can't believe your mom is letting you go back"—came close.

"She *is* letting you go back, isn't she?"

Herculeah didn't answer. Meat thought she was avoiding questions by feigning interest in nature.

"Does she even know you're going?"

"Yes, she knows I'm going. She's giving me one last chance,

mainly because I convinced her that Mr. Hunt would be very disappointed if I didn't show."

"Did she have anything to say about the message?"

"Very little. She did let it slip that she thought it might be one of the Hunts."

"One of them! How many are there?"

"There's a portrait of the family in the hallway and it shows four children, but I could only recognize Shivers Hunt. Mom thinks it might be the older of the sisters. She's been loony for about fifty years."

"Your mom said 'loony'?"

"No, she actually said 'childlike,' but that's what she meant. If it was the sister, Mom said you can't rely on anything she says."

"Like phone messages," Meat said.

"Exactly. Mom said she knows our number and has left messages before—well, parts of messages."

"I don't suppose it could have been Mr. Hunt's voice, because he's paralyzed." A sudden thought crossed his mind. "He *is* paralyzed, isn't he?"

"Yes, he is paralyzed."

"Because you do read about things like this happening. Someone pretends to be paralyzed and then when nobody's looking, they get up and do things." He warmed to the thought. "For all we know, he could have made the threatening phone call."

"He didn't make the call."

"But think of this: He's lying there. You're engrossed in reading to him. You're completely off your guard because the man can't move. Then all of a sudden you hear a sound. You don't pay any attention because the man can't move. Then the sound is closer, but you still don't pay any attention. Then without warning you feel hands around your throat. Now you pay attention but it's too late. Gotcha!"

"Oh, Meat, don't be silly."

"If it's so silly, then why are you rubbing your neck?"

They rounded the corner, and Hunt House lay ahead. They passed through the gates and down the shaded drive.

Meat rang the ding-dong bell, and they waited for a long time before the door was opened.

"You again," Nurse Wegman said.

"Yes."

"Well, you'd better come in." She looked at Meat. "You wait."

Herculeah followed Nurse Wegman up the stairs and went directly to Mr. Hunt's bedroom. "Well, I'm not going to waste any time today," she said, crossing the room and picking up the book. "We are going to read!"

She spoke loudly for Nurse Wegman's benefit. Apparently satisfied by what she had heard, Nurse Wegman left the room.

Herculeah sat and opened the book. "Here's where we were . . . sound of breathing . . . she whispers that she's coming. . . ."

She turned the page. "Oh, I was right. A flashback is coming up." As she straightened, a yellowed piece of paper slipped from the book and fluttered to the floor.

Herculeah said, "Oh, what's this?" She bent and picked it up. "Why, it's a clipping from an old newspaper. Well, part of one. It's been folded in half and unfolded so many times that it's torn. Either that or somebody tore it deliberately."

She opened the book and riffled the pages gently to see if the rest of the clipping would drop out.

"No, I guess this is all there is. . . . Strange."

She held the clipping to the light and, without thinking, began to read aloud.

A family reunion turned to tragedy Saturday afternoon at the Hunt estate. Twenty-five members of the Hunt family had gathered to celebrate the birthday of Lionus Hunt when a children's game—

She broke off. "Oh, I'm so sorry, Mr. Hunt. I wasn't thinking. You probably don't want to hear this. This is your family, isn't it?" She didn't wait for a blink. "You were probably at this party. I'm sure you don't want to relive it."

She paused, and once again she had the feeling that Mr. Hunt was telling her something.

"Or do you?"

One blink. Yes.

"I mean, I know you don't want to relive it—nobody would—but I think you want to hear this, am I right?'

Blink.

"Then we might as well read the rest, or what there is of it. I'll be honest with you. I would like to know about the tragedy. It's not," she went on truthfully, "that I enjoy tragedies, but that I always, always have to know what really happened. Do you want me to read on?"

And although she knew the answer, she waited.

Blink.

"Here goes."

IT CAME FROM THE TOWER

Meat got up from the steps and stretched. He felt he had been sitting here on these stone steps for hours.

He looked at his watch. Only fifteen minutes had passed. Shaking his arm, he tried to rouse the watch and remind it that it had better keep the right time or else.

He walked a few steps away from the house. He bent and pretended to tie his shoe. His shoe did not need tying, of course—the straps were Velcro—but he needed to glance up and see if the scary lady was watching him from the window.

But the windows were empty. Even so, Meat thought, they had the look of eyes—blind eyes, perhaps. He shuddered.

The tower was to the right of the house. Meat glanced at it, examining it. Why, he wondered, was Herculeah so fascinated by it? He moved closer for a better look.

And, his thoughts continued, she really was fascinated. When she had first seen the tower today she had said, "When I see that tower, I feel as if I'm waiting for something to happen, something unknown, something I can't even imagine, something I can't understand." Then she added firmly, "That I can't understand yet!"

He still didn't understand why anyone would want to put one of these hideous things on their house. The house was hideous, too, of course, but that was no reason to put a tower on it.

Again he glanced up at the house, his eyes focusing on the window. He thought he saw a movement there; he waited for a long time, but no face appeared.

Turning his attention back to the tower, he thought about the tragedy that had happened here. It would be nice if he could discover what that tragedy was before Herculeah did.

He heard a noise overhead and looked up, startled.

Birds were flying out of the tower, through the slotted windows, their wings beating fast. They were struggling for their lives as if something were after them.

The sun was in Meat's eyes, and he put one hand up to shield them. Now it seemed that the last of the birds were free from the tower. They had gotten away from whatever had startled them.

Meat took one step closer. Something else was coming out of the tower, but he couldn't make it out. What was that? A stick? Surely it couldn't be an arm.

Then he heard a laugh. It was faint, muted by the thick tower walls, but it could only have come from one throat—that of the woman who had looked down at him from the window.

In his mind he saw it again, the face that had haunted his dreams for two nights, even appearing in his bathroom window, which was a double shock since his bathroom had no window. No wonder the birds were frightened.

Now he could make out that other object coming out of the tower. It was an arm, and at the end of the arm was a hand that was just as he had described to Herculeah. Talons—the hand had talons instead of fingers.

And something was clutched in those terrible talons. It was something round. A stone? Could it be a stone? Why hold a stone out the tower window? Was she going to throw it? The only person she could possibly want to hit with a stone was—

He looked around the empty yard. Him. Him!

Meat gasped. He wanted to run. It was the only sensible thing to do. But he seemed to be rooted to the spot, as unable to move as Mr. Hunt was upstairs in his bed.

The arm lifted. It was the movement a pitcher might make to test the weight of the ball.

Then, in a movement so quick that he almost missed it, the stone left the hand. It was on its way to—to him!

Still he could not move. He was like a rabbit frozen in the headlights of an oncoming car.

The stone fell with surprising slowness. Meat imagined that this was because his heart had sped up a thousand times. He'd read about this. A person's whole life really could pass before his eyes when the heart sped up a thousand times.

The limbs of the trees around him were moved by a sudden gust of wind. Leaves rustled, branches cracked. The wind was so sudden it seemed unearthly, like the woman in the tower.

If the stone tried to go this way or that way, the wind would correct it and send it . . . to him!

Then the stone seemed to flutter as if it had suddenly sprouted wings. That would not have surprised Meat. Nothing would ever surprise him again. Wind, wings, whatever—that stone was going where it was intended to go.

Whoever had thrown the stone was shouting something, but Meat couldn't make it out.

A cry cut through the late afternoon air, drowning out all other sound.

Meat knew that cry even though he had never heard anything like it before. It was the cry of someone about to die.

And it had come from his throat.

10

HALF A TRAGEDY

Herculeah lifted her head.

"Did you hear something?"

She glanced at Mr. Hunt. He was staring at the ceiling, eyes open. There was no response.

"I thought I heard a scream."

Still no response.

Herculeah smiled. "I guess I'm hearing things now." She lifted the clipping.

"Okay, here goes." But she paused a moment, listening. She knew she had heard a scream, and the scream had been somehow familiar. Now there was nothing.

"Well, on to the clipping."

She felt the thrill she always felt when she was on the edge of discovery. Also, there was something about old newspaper clippings that excited her. The writing was more polished back when this piece was written. People respected the news back then and so did the writers who recorded it.

She showed her respect by clearing her throat. She read in a voice that would have won her an audition on prime-time evening news.

A family reunion turned to tragedy Saturday afternoon at the Hunt estate. Twenty-five members of the Hunt family had gathered to celebrate the birthday of Lionus Hunt when a children's game of hide-and-seek ended in death. According to a family spokesman, the adults were in the dining room when they heard screams. They rushed outside and discovered the body of Eleanor Pitman, the children's governess, at the base of the tower. She had been struck on the head by a stone from the tower. Speculation was that the stone had worked loose over the years. No children were hiding in the tower at the time, as the tower door is always locked. This is the second time tragedy has struck the Hunt tower—

"And that's all there is," Herculeah said.

She looked closely at the man on the bed. His eyes were bright with intelligence and . . . something else Herculeah did not understand. Slyness? Cruelty? Interest?

At any rate, Herculeah was sure he knew far more about the story than the newspaper reporter had.

"Were you there at the party?"

Yes.

"Were you part of the game?"

Yes.

"You could tell me what the rest of the clipping said. I know you could—probably word for word. But you know what? I can go to the library. I can look this up. I can find the other half of the tragedy and—"

At that moment Herculeah heard a noise outside in the hallway. It was too soon for the nurse, wasn't it?

She listened. Someone was running in the hallway. The footsteps were light, too soft to be from Nurse Wegman's heavy shoes. The footsteps stopped outside the door.

Herculeah glanced at the man on the bed. She could tell that he recognized the footsteps and knew who waited in the hall.

"Who's there?" Herculeah called.

Then the door to the bedroom opened slowly, creaking on its hinges. Herculeah swirled in her chair.

The face looking at her from the doorway, the face framed in wild hair, was the face of an old woman—something out of a Greek tragedy, something out of a nightmare. Excitement burned in the dark eyes. The cheeks were flushed with something like triumph.

Herculeah knew instantly that this was the face Meat had seen at the window the other day. And she knew instantly why it had filled him with dread.

The woman took one step into the room. Her body was small

and frail. Her hair flew about her head. Her skeletal arms flapped excitedly at her sides.

"It happened again," she said. She punctuated her sentence with a nervous giggle.

"What? What's happened again?"

"Death from the tower."

"What are you talking about? Tell me!"

The woman in the doorway seemed to be smiling, although Herculeah knew this was nothing to smile about. The woman's teeth were dark and as pointed as an animal's. Herculeah's anxiety grew.

Herculeah glanced down at the clipping in her hand. "Are you talking about this?"

She lifted the clipping and showed it to the woman.

The woman shook her head. She had not come here to read a piece of paper. "Again," she said.

"Today? Now?"

Herculeah tried to calm herself with the thought that her mother said you couldn't rely on this old woman, but it didn't work.

The woman took one quick breath before she explained.

"Death fell from the tower." Then as if she was saving the best for last, she added, "The body lies in its shadow."

11

THE BODY IN THE SHADOWS

For a moment Herculeah stared at the old woman, hoping to make sense of the situation. She turned to the man lying so still on the bed, as if he could help her.

She was struck by the fact that their faces were almost identical. Both resembled birds of prey. Their eyes seemed to be looking for something weaker to devour. Her feeling of impending doom heightened.

Then the woman spoke again, her voice rising with excitement. "A body! A body!"

"Whose body?"

"The boy."

Now Herculeah remembered the scream. There had been something familiar about it.

"Meat! Meat!"

Herculeah leaped to her feet. The book dropped to the floor unnoticed.

In the doorway, the woman—childlike—clapped her hands together as if in triumph.

Herculeah ran to the door. The old woman stood there, her hawklike eyes gleaming, her hands clasped together in delight, but Herculeah slipped past her in one quick move.

She ran out into the hall. She crossed quickly to the stairs.

Behind her the old woman let out a squeal of success. Her cackle of delight followed Herculeah down the long stairs.

Nurse Wegman came out of a room down the hall, bringing with her the faint odor of tobacco. "What's wrong?" she asked. "Mr. Hunt?"

"No! Meat!"

She was taking the steps two, three at a time, pulling herself along by the banister. Nurse Wegman was right behind her, matching her speed.

"Your friend?"

"Yes. That old woman said something fell on him from the tower."

"That old fool."

"I thought the tower was locked."

"It is, but there are keys around if you know where to look."

"She said there was a body."

Nurse Wegman was fast, but not as fast as Herculeah, in crossing the hallway. It was Herculeah who got to the front door first. She threw it open and burst out into the late afternoon sun. She turned immediately toward the tower and broke into a run.

"In the shadow of the tower," the old woman had said. Herculeah's eyes scanned the shadows.

"There," said Nurse Wegman.

She passed Herculeah. Herculeah continued to run, but her pace was slowed by her increasing dread.

Meat lay facedown on the ground. His pale face was pressed into what had once been a lawn. He was not moving. He did not even seem to be breathing.

"Oh, no," Herculeah sighed.

"I'll turn him over."

"Maybe you shouldn't move him," Herculeah began, forgetting she was talking to a nurse.

Nurse Wegman turned him over in a quick, unnurselike way, and Meat's face was turned to the sky. The shadow of the tower lay across his pale cheeks.

"Resuscitation!" Herculeah cried, gaining strength. "Mouth-to-mouth resuscitation! Let me! I've had a course. You go call for an ambulance and the police."

"That will not be necessary."

"It is necessary. Get out of my way. We've got to save him! Go call for an ambulance!"

But Nurse Wegman's hands were firm on Herculeah's shoulders, and she could not break free.

"Trust me," Nurse Wegman said, "that will not be necessary."

12

THE KISS OF DEATH

"What do you mean it's not necessary? What do you mean?"

"Don't get hysterical."

"But what do you mean?"

"I mean he's not dead."

These were the most beautiful words Meat had ever heard in his life. He had been lying there wondering about that very thing. He didn't know where he was except that it was somewhere he didn't want to be.

His face had been pressed into grass that had seen better days when he felt himself being turned over. Bits and pieces of memory began to come to him. He had heard Herculeah's voice, so she was here. Also that nurse—whatever her name was—and then he remembered hearing Herculeah saying something about mouth-to-mouth resuscitation.

That had been a sort of fantasy of Meat's. He could not imagine kissing Herculeah, but he could, in a particularly wild dream, imagine something like mouth-to-mouth as an emergency measure. The kiss of death, he thought of it, not unpleasantly.

Then he remembered Nurse Wegman. She had flipped him over—he thought with her foot—and he realized with a real sense of horror that if any lips were going to come in contact with his, they would be Nurse Wegman's.

Meat opened his eyes.

"Hello," he said.

"He *is* alive!" Herculeah cried. There was such joy in her voice that, despite all the horror he had endured, his spirits rose like sun breaking through black clouds.

"I think he just fainted," Nurse Wegman said. "His pulse is normal. I see no injuries. I'll elevate his legs."

"No, no, I'm all right," Meat said. He wanted his legs to stay right where they were—stretched out on the ground. "Just let me lie here for a moment."

"What happened, Meat? Can you tell us?"

"I was walking toward the tower, just checking things out, and all of a sudden, birds came flying out of the windows, like they'd been startled."

"Take it easy," Nurse Wegman advised, as if she was making an effort to be a nurse. "Take deep breaths. Speak slowly."

"And I saw an arm—"

Now Nurse Wegman stopped sounding like a disinterested nurse. "You saw an arm? An arm in the tower?"

"Well, it was like an arm—a skeleton arm. Maybe it was a stick, but it looked like an arm."

"So someone was in the tower."

"Yes."

Herculeah thought of the old woman. She remembered the thin, sticklike arms, fluttering in the air, clapping with delight.

"And then there was something in the hand—so it had to be an arm if there was a hand attached."

"Death fell from the tower," Herculeah said, remembering the old woman's words. She glanced at Nurse Wegman. "That's what the old woman said it was."

"It looked like a stone to me," Meat said.

"Go on," Nurse Wegman ordered.

"And then she threw the stone, or whatever it was, at me. I wasn't worried at first because I was standing back here. And I knew that nobody could throw a stone that far, especially an old woman."

Nurse Wegman took a deep breath. "I've got to get back to my patient." She turned quickly, crossed the yard, and disappeared into the house.

"I'm glad she's gone," Meat said. "I don't think she likes me."

"She doesn't like anybody. Go on."

"Only whatever she threw came at me, like, in slow motion. It was as if it were on a radar course or something and I knew it was going to hit me. I knew I was going to die."

"Why didn't you run?"

"I couldn't."

"What did you do?"

"I screamed."

"And then?"

"You know the rest?"

"I don't! And then what?"

"Then I fainted."

13

FLYING FINISH

"It has to be here somewhere," Herculeah said.

She was walking up and down in front of the tower. Meat was sitting where he had fallen, watching her.

"Because, Meat, stones do not just disappear."

"No," Meat agreed.

Herculeah's sharp eyes went over every inch of the ground. "If it rolled," she said, more to herself than to Meat, "then it would have ended up here. But"—she shrugged—"there's nothing."

Meat was beginning to feel uneasy. In thinking back to the moment when the stone—and he had thought it was a stone, then; at any rate, it had been round—had appeared, Meat realized he didn't know exactly what he had seen.

"The sun was in my eyes," he explained.

"Well, yeah, but you saw her throw something, right?"

"Right."

Herculeah moved closer. Her gray eyes had that look that seemed to penetrate right into his brain.

"Go over it again. Describe what you saw."

"Well, it was round. When it left her hand, it was round—I'm sure of that. And then it was as if, I don't know, it sort of sprouted wings."

"Wings! Like a bird?"

Meat drew in a deep, unhappy breath. "I know you wouldn't understand."

"I want to understand. I've got to, because I know that whatever she threw had some meaning and that if we could find it, we would know—"

She broke off. Meat glanced quickly up at the tower, thinking Herculeah had seen something at one of the windows. He struggled to his feet and took a few unsteady steps backward.

"Is the old woman back?" he asked.

"No," Herculeah answered. "But I just remembered where she probably is. She was outside Mr. Hunt's room, and I bet she went inside. I ran off and left Mr. Hunt at the mercy of that woman. Nurse Wegman did, too."

Meat felt a pang of sympathy for the man. Being in the same world with that loony woman was bad enough; being in the same room would be unbearable. And the man was paralyzed. He couldn't protect himself. Meat took another backward step to get away from the thought.

"I've got to make sure he's all right. You keep looking for the—whatever it is we're looking for. Don't leave."

Meat could not have gone anywhere if he had wanted to, and he did want very much to go somewhere—home. But he would settle for any place that didn't have a tower. He glanced around without enthusiasm at his possibilities.

Herculeah ran to the house. The front door stood open as if Nurse Wegman had had the same thought as Herculeah—Mr. Hunt's safety.

Herculeah ran into the hallway and up the stairs. She took them three at a time. She crossed the hall and came to a stop in the doorway to Mr. Hunt's bedroom.

Nurse Wegman was beside the bed. She was leaning over Mr. Hunt's body, a pillow in one hand.

"Is he all right?" Herculeah asked.

Nurse Wegman straightened abruptly. She looked around, obviously startled. She punched the pillow with one hand, as if to make it more comfortable, and then settled it under Mr. Hunt's head.

"He's fine. The old woman was in here. She was by the bed, holding this pillow. I thought she was getting ready to smother him."

Herculeah crossed to the bed and stood beside the nurse. She looked down into the bright hawklike eyes.

"I'm sorry I ran out like that," she said, speaking to Mr. Hunt. "My friend fainted outside and that . . . that woman who was in here—your sister, I guess—must have thought he was dead. I don't know if you want me to come back or not, after the way I've acted."

The blink came forcefully. Yes.

"Good. I want to come back. I'm going to redeem myself." She picked up the book, slipped the newspaper clipping inside, and put it on the bedside table. "Next time we will do nothing but read."

Herculeah paused. One hand still rested on the book. She had the feeling that Mr. Hunt wanted to tell her something, needed to tell her something important. He needs my help, she thought abruptly, and not just to read him books.

Nurse Wegman coughed to remind her to leave. When that didn't work, she said, "Go on now. Look after your friend. Mr. Hunt needs to rest."

"I'm on my way." At the doorway she paused. "I wonder if I could use the phone. I need to call my mom."

"We don't need any private detectives around here."

"No, but Meat and I are going to need a ride home. I don't think he can make it on foot."

"The phone's downstairs in the hall."

"Thanks. I'll see you both tomorrow?"

She glanced at Nurse Wegman, hoping for many reasons that it wouldn't be Nurse Wegman's day to be on duty.

But to her disappointment, Nurse Wegman said firmly, "I'll be here," and then added, "from now on."

14

MIRROR IMAGE

"I'm phoning my mom to come pick us up," Herculeah called to Meat from the front door.

Meat turned toward her. His lips moved, and although she could not quite make out his words, Herculeah suspected they were something like, "That's the first good idea you've had all day."

With one quick glance at the tower she disappeared back into the house.

Meat watched her go. Then with slow steps he began to make his way to the porch.

Herculeah glanced around the hall for the telephone. The hall was large, high-ceilinged, and dark. All the rooms in Hunt House, she thought, seemed to be shadowed in gloom, as if they had secrets to hide.

There. Herculeah found the phone at the back of the hall, in one of those gloomy shadows.

It was an old-timey black rotary phone, and as she picked it up, she shook her head. She had to dial the number. Dial! This was probably the first time she had ever not punched in the numbers.

She dialed and shifted from one foot to the other, waiting impatiently for the phone to be answered.

All of a sudden Herculeah had the feeling she was being watched. It was such a strong feeling that she glanced first at the portrait of Lionus Hunt. She smiled at her foolishness. Of course no hawklike eyes peered at her through slits in the painted eyes.

She turned slowly. She thought her hair was beginning to frizzle. She found herself looking into an old mirror. The glass was wavery with age, and so at first all she could make out was her own hair. Yes, it was definitely frizzling. Then she noticed a figure crouching behind her on the stairs.

She tried to breathe slowly, deeply to calm herself. The phone rang twice. Pick up, Mom, she said to herself. I'm in trouble here.

Now she could hear, above the ringing of the phone, the beginning of a childish giggle. It was low, broken by mutterings of the woman reminding herself to be more quiet.

Pick up, Mom. I need you.

A hand came through the banisters, reaching for her. The long-taloned fingers curled as if to grab. "Pretty," she said. The fingers brushed her hair, and the old woman said, "Come closer."

No way, Herculeah said to herself, and she moved away from the stairs. She was almost against the wall now. But she was in a better position to make a beeline for the door if that became necessary.

Answer me, Mom. Answer.

On the fourth ring, as if in answer to Herculeah's pleas, her mother's voice came on the line.

"Hello. You have reached the office of Mim Jones. I cannot take your call right now, but if you leave a message and phone number at the beep, I'll get back to you as soon as I can."

The beep came and Herculeah said, "Mom, it's me. I'm at Hunt House. We've had a bit of excitement. I'm fine but Meat fainted, and I need you to come out and pick us up. Now."

She waited because sometimes, when her mother was busy, she wouldn't answer her phone, but she always answered when she heard Herculeah's voice, especially when it was something urgent.

Her mother did not answer now, and Herculeah reluctantly hung up the phone.

"I've got to make one more quick call," she said. She glanced up at the woman and then toward the front porch where Meat sat on the steps. "You aren't going to like this one, Meat," she predicted as she dialed.

The phone was answered on the second ring this time, and Herculeah gave her message.

She glanced at the stairs. "Well, our ride is on the way; it'll probably be here any minute."

The skeleton arm still reached through the banisters, the long fingers stretching for Herculeah's hair. And if it frizzled any more, Herculeah thought, she'd get it.

Quickly she returned the phone to the table and backed away from the stairs. "I'll wait outside."

The fingers closed on air, and then the old woman spoke. It was as if she had awakened from a dream, as if she had been so dazzled by Herculeah's hair that she had forgotten her mission.

"Did you find it?" she asked in a tired whisper.

"What?"

"Did you?"

"Did I find what you threw from the tower? Is that what you want to know?"

"Yes."

"No. What did you throw? Why?"

But the woman seemed to be fading, to be shrinking.

"I don't know." Then she had one final burst of energy. "When you find it, you will know," she said.

She got to her feet and, holding the banister, began to pull herself up the stairs.

"Wait." Now it was Herculeah who reached through the banisters, her fingers brushing the worn fabric of the woman's dress as she moved out of range. "Wait."

The woman shook her head. She chuckled to herself and disappeared onto the landing.

"It's not funny," Herculeah said to the empty hallway. Then she sighed and walked to the door.

THE FOURTH FAINT

"I just had a talk with the woman who threw something at you from the tower," Herculeah told Meat.

"You actually talked to her?"

"Yes."

"She admitted she threw something?"

"Yes."

"So what was it?"

"The most intelligent thing I got out of her was that when we find it, we will know what it is."

"Great. So is your mom coming?" Meat asked.

"Our ride is on the way, Meat. Sit down." She patted the step beside her.

"Your mom is coming, right? You didn't—"

To divert Meat, Herculeah said quickly, "You know, Meat, you really ought to do something about your fainting. You faint all the time."

He was diverted. "I do not."

"Well," Herculeah said, "you fainted that time at Madame Rosa's."

Meat said, "Yes," quickly, hoping that would end the story.

"You were sitting out in the hall," Herculeah recounted, "and you thought the murderer was coming down the stairs—"

"The murderer *was* coming down the stairs."

"Yes, it was the murderer, but you thought it was Madame Rosa's ghost. That's why you fainted."

Meat said, "Getting back to our ride . . ."

Herculeah said, "Then there was that time you were in the park and you thought some boys were going to punch you in the stomach."

"They *were* going to punch me in the stomach."

"But they didn't have to, because you fainted."

Why was she doing this, Meat wondered, bringing up his fainting? Was she trying to divert him? Oh, yes—the ride!

He heard a car turn into the driveway, looked up, and gave a gasp of dismay.

"Oh, here she is," Herculeah said cheerfully.

"It's my mom. You said you were calling *your* mom."

"I couldn't get her."

"You didn't tell Mom I fainted."

"I had to, or she wouldn't have come. Hi, Mrs. Mac," Herculeah called as she went down the steps. "Thanks for coming."

As he followed, Meat hissed, "Let me tell it."

Meat flung the door open. He said, "I don't care what she said, Mom, I did not faint." He got into the backseat and slammed the door.

Herculeah had known he wouldn't be pleased, but he had never slammed the door in her face before. She opened the door and said, "Scoot over."

At least he wasn't too mad to scoot over, and Herculeah climbed in beside him. Meat's mom turned around and gave her son a hard look. "So," she said, "if you didn't faint, what did happen?"

"Nothing! I was standing outside looking up at the tower and birds started flying out the windows. And then an arm came and threw something and somebody yelled something and—"

"You didn't tell me she yelled something," Herculeah interrupted.

"I couldn't hear what it was—probably something stupid like 'Look up here!' Where else would anybody be looking?" He paused. "Anyway, I got dizzy. Looking up like that always makes me dizzy. I sat down, put my head between my knees, and was fine."

Mrs. Mac's gaze turned to Herculeah, so she knew it was her turn.

"I was in the house when this happened, Mrs. Mac, so I didn't see it. I had found this old newspaper clipping. It was in the back of the book I was reading to Mr. Hunt. It was a clipping about a tragedy years ago at Hunt House and guess what the tragedy was?"

"Someone threw a stone from the tower and killed the governess," Mrs. McMannis said.

"Yes! Exactly! But nobody threw it. It was a loose stone and it fell."

"It was thrown."

"How do you know? The clipping said no one was in the tower."

"Someone was in the tower. There had to have been. My great uncle Ben was the stonemason who worked on the tower. He laid those stones, and he said those stones were laid to stay laid."

"Why would anyone want to kill a governess?"

"Maybe the killer was aiming at someone else. I don't know."

Herculeah looked at Mrs. McMannis sharply. "Who was close to the governess at the time?"

"I have no idea."

"Probably one of the twins," Herculeah said thoughtfully. "The smaller one." Her mind turned back to the family portrait on the stairs, to the figure of the smaller twin that had been damaged somehow.

"Did the article mention that this was the second tragedy?" Mrs. McMannis continued.

"Yes, I was going to the library to look that up."

"A man working on the tower was killed. Ben was there when he fell. No big deal."

"Except to the man who fell," Herculeah said, "and his family."

Mrs. Mac didn't care for the comment. "No good can come from that tower or that house. You stay away from that place, Albert." She turned the key and started the car.

"He has to come, Mrs. Mac," Herculeah told the back of her head. "It wouldn't be any fun without him."

Meat looked at her in amazement. Fun? Hunt House was fun? He read the answer in her face. She thought it was fun, like something in an amusement park where no danger is real.

As if the matter was settled Herculeah said, "Here's what we've got to do tomorrow. Something was thrown at you from the tower, and it wasn't a stone."

"No."

"And," Herculeah continued, "I don't think it was anything that would have done you harm. I think the old woman was trying to tell you something or warn you of something."

"Why me?"

"Maybe because she needed someone and you were there. We're getting close. Whatever fell from the tower is the answer to the mystery. We've got to find it."

Mrs. McMannis glanced at Herculeah in the rearview mirror and smiled sweetly. Herculeh never trusted Mrs. Mac when she smiled like that.

"Oh, Albert won't be able to go with you tomorrow."

Herculeah said quickly, "You don't have to worry about him, Mrs. Mac, I'll be with him every second."

"No, I won't worry about him." Now her smile changed as she looked at Meat, but Herculeah didn't trust that smile, either. "Albert, guess who called this afternoon. And it wasn't Steffie."

Now she looked at Herculeah. They were stopped at a red light now, so Meat's mom was free to smile triumphantly without causing a wreck. "I'm not sure you remember Steffie, Herculeah. She's that girl that was visiting and was so crazy about Albert."

"I remember Steffie."

"Anyway, it wasn't Steffie this time. Albert, it was your dad. You need to stay home tomorrow so you won't miss the call."

The light changed. The car moved forward, but the three people inside had nothing more to say.

16

THE THINK COCOON

Herculeah took out her granny glasses. She put them on, hooking the thin metal wires behind her ears.

Herculeah had gotten these glasses at Hidden Treasures, a secondhand store where she often shopped. Herculeah bought some of her clothes there, and other useful things. Once when she had been in Hidden Treasures, she had tried on these glasses. She couldn't see anything out of them, but she discovered she could think better. The world seemed to blur into a mist, making her ideas stand out. "It's like being in a think cocoon," she had explained to Meat.

She was sitting on her bed, waiting for her thoughts to clear when her mother came and stood in the doorway.

"Have you got on those ridiculous glasses again?" her mother said. "You're going to ruin your eyes."

Herculeah couldn't see her mom, but she knew she was there. She pushed the glasses to the top of her head.

"Hi, Mom."

"So what was the phone message about? Why did you need me to come pick you up?"

"Oh, that. I meant to erase it. Meat's mom came and got us. It was nothing. Meat fainted."

"Fainted?"

"Oh, Mom, he faints all the time."

"I didn't know that. So what was the excitement you mentioned?"

"Meat was standing out in the yard and someone threw something out of the tower window, and Meat got dizzy watching it and fainted. End of story."

Herculeah sincerely hoped it was.

"Someone was in the tower?"

"Yes, the sister."

"I thought it was locked."

"The new nurse said there are keys if you know where to look."

"How would she know that? The woman's only been there one day."

"Good question."

"I'll have to talk to the lawyer. There's been enough tragedy connected with that tower."

"I know. Meat's mom told us. Someone threw a stone from the tower and killed the governess." She eyed her mother, pretending to be critical. "You could take some lessons from Mrs. Mac."

Her mom knew Herculeah's opinion of Mrs. Mac. She smiled. "How so?"

"She tells us things. For example, if she knew what you were working on for Mr. Hunt, she would tell us. She doesn't treat everything as a big secret."

Her mom seemed to think that over. "Mr. Randolph, the lawyer, was drawing up a will for Mr. Hunt. This was before his stroke, and he wanted some investigative work done. He contacted me. I was to find the other sister. That was the extent of my involvement, but I became interested in the old man. I felt sorry for him. I used to drop in and see him from time to time."

"This sister you were going to find. It's not the old crazy one who left the message on your machine."

"No. There were younger sisters—twins. Only one of them is alive now, and that was who I was to find."

Herculeah had her mom talking now, and she didn't want her to stop. "Everybody says there's money hidden in the house—even Nurse Wegman. By the way, I don't trust her. She's weird."

"Mr. Randolph hired the nurses himself. They're the same team that nursed his invalid mother, so you don't have to worry about them."

"So is there money hidden in the house?"

"I hope you haven't been poking around the house looking for it."

"Of course not. Give me some credit. I'm smarter than that."

"Too smart sometimes." Her mother changed the subject. "Did you get supper?"

"I ordered pizza. There's some left if you want it."

"I grabbed a bite on the way home. Incidentally, I'll be leaving early in the morning."

"Don't work too hard."

"I won't."

She left and Herculeah put her granny glasses on again. "Think," she told her brain. "Think about what could have been thrown from the tower. What could have sprouted wings? What—?"

Before her brain had a chance to work, the phone rang. "I'll get it, Mom, it's probably Meat.

"Oh, hi, Meat," she said, "I was hoping it was you. Also, I'm hoping that you'll go to Hunt House with me tomorrow. It won't be any fun without you."

"Didn't you hear what Mom said in the car? My dad's going to call."

"I heard, but if he calls early . . ."

"Maybe."

"Don't you want to find out what was thrown at you?"

"I guess."

"Remember that old song 'Blowin' in the Wind'?" She tried

to make her voice mysterious so he would be interested.

"Yes."

"Well, something was blowin' in the wind at Hunt House."

"And you're going to find out what it was."

"I've got to."

"Call me when you get back."

"I will. Maybe I'll call before I go—try to change your mind. I gotta go now. Good night, Meat."

"Good night."

Herculeah sighed. Maybe she could compete with a phone call from an airhead like Steffie, but not a call from Macho Man. She adjusted her granny glasses and waited, hoping to get an idea of what had been blowin' in the wind.

17

HERCULEAH ON HER OWN

This was the first time Herculeah had come to Hunt House without Meat at her side. She missed him. Being with Meat always made her feel she had to be brave and protective. She didn't want anything to happen to him. And she knew she was going to have to be especially brave today.

The night before, when her mom came in to say a final good night, she had said, "I'd rather you didn't go back to Hunt House to read to Mr. Hunt."

"Mom!"

"At least not until I've had a chance to talk to Mr. Randolph about the situation."

"Mom!"

"And I'll do that tomorrow. Good night, Herculeah."

Her mother had not, Herculeah reminded herself, said, "I forbid you to go to Hunt House." She had said, "I'd rather you didn't go back to Hunt House to read to Mr. Hunt." And she wasn't going to read. She wasn't even going into the house. She was going to clear up a mystery.

The house came into view, and Herculeah had to admit that the house did have a face, and not a welcoming one. She paused inside the open gate. Which was not welcoming, either. It was rather like a Venus flytrap, open to lure in the unwary. See, she told herself, if Meat were here and said something like that, I would make a joke of it.

She continued up the drive to the house.

The day matched her mood—gloomy. The gray arch of the sky overhead was lower today. She felt she could almost reach up and touch the dark patches of clouds.

"It's going to rain," she told herself. Hurrying, she left the gate behind and, as if on cue, something hit the dry ground at her feet. It hit with such a sharp sound that Herculeah thought at first of a bullet.

She glanced down. A raindrop. She smiled at herself.

Meat, I could really use you, she said to herself. This house is getting to me.

The single raindrop was followed by a smattering of them. Herculeah crossed the drive quickly and took shelter in a grove of trees.

She paused. She hadn't heard thunder or seen any lightning, so it didn't seem reckless or unsafe to wait for a few minutes under the trees.

As she waited, she moved slowly toward the tower, keeping

under the protective branches. She felt an odd tingling as she got closer. It was as if she were moving not just closer to the tower but to the solution of its mystery.

And there was a mystery.

She turned her eyes from the tower to the house. There were no signs of life around Hunt House today. There were no lights in the windows, no smoke in the chimney. It reminded Herculeah of the vacation houses at the beach that had been closed for the winter.

Herculeah continued to move closer. Now she could see the very spot where Meat had stood when he had seen something coming toward him from the tower, the exact spot where his body had lain after he had fainted.

Her eyes narrowed in concentration. She began to calculate distances.

But wait a minute, she cautioned herself. Meat had said something about wind. He'd told her that a sudden gust of wind had come up and sent the missile straight toward him.

But nothing had touched him. So whatever it was had to have been carried farther by the wind. Perhaps it had gone over his head.

Her gaze swept over the ground behind where Meat had fallen.

And, she remembered, the missile had been light. It was not stone; Herculeah was sure of that. So if something light was thrown from the tower—a ball of fabric or a balled-up garment, and this ball became unfolded or unwrapped by the wind in the process, well it might have looked like it sprouted wings, as Meat described. . . .

Her thoughts were going so well, Herculeah thought it was as if she had on her granny glasses.

And, her thoughts raced, if this something came unwrapped and was caught by the wind, then it could have gone much, much farther than she had thought.

She began to retrace her steps, keeping close to the trees. The brief rain had stopped, but she somehow sensed that she still needed the protection of the trees.

She glanced at the house. There was still no sign of life there.

These grounds had once been tended and cared for. This had been a beautiful lawn with birdbaths and statues. She came to an overgrown clearing.

In the center of the clearing she could see the ruins of an old fountain. Stones had fallen from the sides. The statue that had once graced the center of the fountain had fallen on its side.

There! She saw what she had been looking for.

It was a brown, stone-colored bundle blown against the fallen statue. It was so much the color of the statue that it was as if it had been deliberately camouflaged.

She approached carefully, looking over her shoulder at the house. No one seemed to be watching, so she bent and picked up the bundle.

It was a large piece of fabric, a garment of some kind, slightly damp now from the recent rain shower. She gathered it up and moved back into the shelter of the trees.

She unfolded the garment and held it up. It was a coat. It was one of those practical all-purpose coats that Herculeah's mother was always after her to buy.

She drew in her breath and peered closer. There were dark stains on the fabric. Brown stains. And Herculeah knew instantly what the stains were.

Blood.

18

DRAGON-LADY RED AND TICKLE-ME PINK

Herculeah felt an instant and deep concern for the owner of this coat. And, at the same time, she felt a deep determination to find out what had happened to the owner.

The belt of the coat hung loosely to the ground. She ran her fingers over it thoughtfully as if seeking a clue.

She realized that if the raincoat had been wrapped and tied with the belt before being thrown from the tower, it would look exactly as Meat had described it. First it would appear to be round, even a stone, and then as it unfolded and was blown by the wind it might seem to have wings.

But whose coat was it?

She held it against her, checking the size. It was a small coat, too small to fit her. And way too small for Nurse Wegman.

She eyed it. And it couldn't belong to the sister. She hadn't been out of the house for fifty years. The style of clothing she wore was so old that even Hidden Treasures wouldn't carry it.

She patted the pockets.

Yes! Now at last she would learn something about the owner of the coat. What people kept in their pockets was often revealing.

She was reaching into the left pocket when she saw movement at the house. Instinctively she drew back deeper into the trees.

The front door opened and Nurse Wegman came out. She was wearing a down jacket and a cap. The peak of the cap hid her eyes.

She paused on the steps and looked to the right and left. Her eyes seemed to linger on the grove of trees where Herculeah was hiding. Herculeah clutched the coat tightly against her as if for protection. To her great relief, the eyes moved on.

Nurse Wegman came down the steps. She turned away from the direction of the tower. Anyway, she couldn't have been headed there. The tower had no outside door. She circled the house and walked to the large stone garage at the rear. Herculeah had not noticed the garage before. Nurse Wegman entered the garage by a side door and closed it behind her.

Herculeah sighed with relief. Now she could get back to the pockets. She reached into the left pocket and took out the contents. There wasn't as much there as she had hoped—a crumpled tissue, a small comb, and a lipstick.

Well, there was one other pocket to search. She was disappointed in what she found there, too—a scarf and a single white glove.

The scarf was white silk. The lipstick was Coty. Herculeah took off the cap and twisted the base. The lipstick was pale pink.

She glanced at the bottom of the tube. In the little red circle, in white letters, was the shade: Petal Rose.

Herculeah didn't know much about lipsticks—she didn't bother with the stuff herself—but she did know that a lipstick called Petal Rose would never have appealed to Nurse Wegman. She'd want something like Dragon-Lady Red.

And the old sister, she'd want something like Tickle-Me Pink. Herculeah grinned. Maybe, she thought, I'll go into the cosmetics business and think of names for them.

She broke off quickly.

She noticed the garage door was being opened. She noticed one other thing: Her hair was beginning to frizzle.

19

DEAD PHONE, DEAD MAN?

The garage door was not one of those modern, remote-controlled garage doors. This door required manpower, but Nurse Wegman was up to the job. She shoved the door with such force that it not only opened but rattled overhead in its tracks as if it didn't want to stop. Herculeah could hear the noise from where she stood in the trees.

A car shot out of the garage. Nurse Wegman was at the wheel.

She backed the car onto the grass and turned onto the drive with such speed that gravel flew. She did not glance in Herculeah's direction. Nurse Wegman seemed to be in a hurry.

Herculeah moved out of the trees to make sure Nurse Wegman drove through the gates. She watched the car disappear around the bend and out of sight.

Herculeah's mind then turned to Mr. Hunt. Had Nurse Wegman left him alone? Was the housekeeper there? The

housekeeper usually parked her car—an old Buick—by the kitchen door.

Holding the coat against her, Herculeah went around the house. As she had feared, there was no car parked by the door.

I've got to call Mom, Herculeah thought. This situation has gotten out of hand. Mr. Hunt has been abandoned.

She tried the kitchen door. It was locked. She knocked and peered through the glass. She saw no one, and no one came to the door.

She went quickly around the house. She paused at the window of the library. The curtains had been opened, and she looked in. She saw a scene of destruction. All the books lay on the floor. Pictures had been torn from the walls.

With a sinking feeling, Herculeah continued to the front of the house. She went up the steps, draped the raincoat over a porch chair, and turned the doorbell. The ding-dong of doom—as Meat called it—sounded, but no one came to answer. She turned the doorknob, but the door was locked.

"Hello, is anybody home?"

She had turned to go when suddenly she heard a faint click. It was as if someone had done something to the lock of the door. Herculeah reached out and took the doorknob a second time. Now it turned in her hand.

She pushed, and the huge door opened. The hall inside was empty. No one was in sight. Perhaps, Herculeah thought, the door had been unlocked all along.

She was not satisfied with this explanation, but she couldn't waste time wondering about it. She went directly to the phone at the back of the hall. She would call her mom, and then she would leave Hunt House. She would take herself out of what was becoming an increasingly frightening situation.

She put one hand up to her hair. My hair is too frightened to even frizzle, she thought, trying to make herself smile.

She stopped at the telephone table where yesterday she had called her mom. The phone was not there. It had been overturned and lay beneath the table on the floor. Herculeah picked up the phone and listened. The line was dead.

She glanced around in confusion. Maybe, she thought, that was why Nurse Wegman had left in such a hurry. Maybe something had happened upstairs and Mr. Hunt needed attention. Nurse Wegman had had to go and phone for the doctor. Or an ambulance!

Herculeah glanced overhead at the ceiling as if she could find the answer there. Then, making a quick decision, she ran to the stairs. Taking them in twos, then threes, she was soon at the top.

"Mr. Hunt!"

She ran to his bedroom. The door was open.

"Mr. Hunt!"

Herculeah rushed into the room. Today the air was stale with the odor of sickness. As she crossed to the high bed, she saw that the sheets had not been changed. Mr. Hunt wore the same stained gown from yesterday.

She glanced around. The curtains had been drawn over the windows. It seemed more like a funeral parlor than a sick room.

Mr. Hunt lay without moving. His eyes were dull and listless and stared up at the ceiling. Herculeah saw no sign of life.

"Mr. Hunt, it's me, Herculeah Jones."

His thin arms lay palm-up on either side of his body. Gently she reached out and touched the inside of his wrist. She had a moment of relief as she felt his faint pulse. He was not dead.

She bent closer, and now she could hear him breathing. It was shallow, however, and his face was pale.

"Mr. Hunt, can you hear me?"

She froze. For in that moment, when her guard was down, she heard a noise in the hallway behind her.

A footstep.

Someone was there.

The softness, the stealth of the footstep told Herculeah that whoever was outside did not want her to know they were there.

Herculeah waited. Her heart pounded with fear. She was frozen in place at Mr. Hunt's bedside. She listened with increasing dread for the next, closer footstep.

THE KEY

Minutes passed, clicked off audibly by the old clock in the hall downstairs.

Herculeah did not move. She listened, her face turned toward the doorway, her heart in her throat.

She heard no more footsteps.

Moving carefully, quietly, Herculeah crossed to the door. She peered out. The hall was empty. She stepped outside the door and looked both ways. There was no one in sight. As she turned to go back into the room, she glanced down at her feet.

There lay a key.

It was an old iron key, heavy. It was the kind of key that would open a basement door, a garage door, or—she drew in her breath—the door to a tower.

She tried to remember if the key had been there when she had come up the stairs. She didn't think so, but it could have been. She had been in such a hurry, she could have stepped right over it and not noticed.

She picked up the key and held it in her hand, feeling the weight of it. Her fingers curled around the metal as she reentered Mr. Hunt's bedroom.

Mr. Hunt's eyes still stared blindly at the ceiling.

"I need your help, Mr. Hunt," she said.

She opened her fingers and held the key in front of his unseeing eyes.

"Mr. Hunt," she said. Her voice was low with urgency. "I need your help, Mr. Hunt. I need to know if this is the key to the tower."

No answer.

"Just blink once if it is. I have to know."

No answer.

"Mr. Hunt, please try to help me. I found this key outside the door to your room. It was on the floor. I think someone put it there deliberately. I think someone wanted me to find it."

No answer.

"Because if this is the key to the tower, I think it means that someone wants me to go there. There's something there that I'm supposed to see, something important."

She was talking to herself now. "And there's no door to the tower outside, so this key opens a door that's somewhere inside the house." She turned back to Mr. Hunt.

"Is there something in the tower, Mr. Hunt? Something I ought to see?"

She glanced at the drawn curtains as if to see beyond them to the tower. Then she looked over her shoulder at the door.

"Because this is beginning to make sense to me. When I tried the front door, it was locked. Then there was a faint click and the door opened. It was as if someone wanted to me to come in. Then when I was beside your bed, I heard a footstep. No one appeared, but this key was left where I would find it. Someone is telling me to go to the tower."

She continued to hold the key in front of Mr. Hunt's unblinking, unseeing eyes.

"Is this the key to the tower, Mr. Hunt? And if so, should I go there?"

His eyes closed, then opened.

"Oh, that was stupid. I asked two questions. You'll have to do it again because I don't know if that was just a reflex or if you were telling me, yes, this is the key to the tower and, yes, I should go there."

Mr. Hunt had no more answers to give, and Herculeah wasn't sure that one blink had been an answer.

"Mr. Hunt, I know it's your sister who is trying to lead us to the tower. Yesterday she threw a woman's coat from the tower. Today, this key. She is determined that someone will go there. And there is no one left to go but me."

Herculeah made her decision.

"I'll be back," she told Mr. Hunt. She started for the doorway, crossed the hall, and ran down the stairs.

She paused for a moment at the foot of the stairs and glanced at the front door. All her instincts told her that she should leave now. She should go out the door while she still could. She should get help.

But the key. The key!

Mr. Hunt's sister had given her this key as surely as if she had put it directly into her hands. The sister had wanted her to come into the house and now wanted her to unlock the door to the tower.

And if she left, her thoughts continued, whatever was in the tower might disappear. If she left, she would never know the secret it held. That was something Herculeah could not bear.

She didn't know where the door to the tower was, but she knew the direction. She ran through the hall, through an old parlor, into another hallway. The first nurse had said a person could get lost in the house. She said there were odd-shaped rooms and halls that led nowhere.

This was one of those halls that led nowhere. Herculeah turned. There was a small storage room on the left, then another hallway. It was like a maze. The door had to be here somewhere.

With the key clasped tightly in her hand, she continued her frantic search for the tower's entrance.

21

AT THE WINDOW

Meat was standing at his living-room window. He had been standing here ever since Herculeah had left for Hunt House. His dad had not called, and Meat was not free to leave until he did.

He had already been uneasy about her going, but there had been something in her early morning phone call that had made him even more uneasy. "I wish you were going with me," she had said. The voice had not sounded like Herculeah at all.

"I wish I could, too," he had said. It wasn't true; what he really wanted was for neither of them to go again—ever. He'd blurted out, "Don't go!"

And she had answered, as he had known she would, "I have to."

There at the window, Meat would occasionally rub his hands nervously up and down his sweatshirt. As he did this, he thought of all the dangers, all the things that could harm her.

There was Mr. Hunt. Meat wasn't at all sure the man was

really paralyzed. The thought of Herculeah sitting there, unaware, reading that terrible book when suddenly . . . gotcha!

Meat swallowed.

The sound was loud enough to reach his mother in the kitchen. "Are you all right, Albert?" she called.

"I'm fine."

Then there was the old woman. He had looked into her face and seen madness and evil, and the thought of Herculeah being trapped by her in one of those dark rooms . . .

He swallowed again. Immediately he called out, "I'm still fine," to his mother.

He realized then that he was trying to swallow his fear. He knew from past experience that fear was an object that could not be swallowed.

Then there was Nurse Wegman. Meat had only seen her for a moment or two at the front door and when he was recovering from a faint, but there had been a look in her eyes that he hadn't liked. It reminded him of a newspaper picture he'd seen of a nurse who went around killing old people, putting them out of their misery.

What was it they had called her? Oh, yes—"The Angel of Death."

Meat didn't even try to swallow that thought. He just pressed his fingers against his throat to hold the terror from rising any higher.

And then there was the tower.

The tower was a place where tragedy happened. It had happened twice before, and it would happen again. He himself had almost been the victim, but a tower like that would not be satisfied with only two victims.

Meat's mom came and stood in the doorway to the living room. She smelled nicely of barbecued pork chops, but Meat, whose throat was blocked, could not have eaten anything.

"If you're so worried about Herculeah . . ." she began.

Meat didn't let her finish. "I didn't say I was worried about her."

"You didn't have to. If you're so worried about Herculeah, why don't you call her?"

"She's at Hunt House."

"Well. Hunt House has a phone, doesn't it? She called me on it yesterday to ask for a ride."

"Mom, that's not a bad idea." He sighed. "Only it's probably an unlisted number."

"It's not. I looked it up." She handed him a Post-it note with a number on it.

"Why are you doing this?" he asked, genuinely puzzled by this unexpected kindness.

"Sometimes I think I'm a little hard on the girl. I actually felt sorry for her yesterday when we were talking about Steffie. She isn't entirely to blame for the way she is. She's got a private detective for a mother and a police detective for a father. I'm not saying a word against the father—we owe a debt of gratitude to him. He saved your uncle Neiman."

"And he found my father," Meat added.

She gave him a sharp look. "A phone call to Hunt House is one thing. I don't want you to go back there. Is that clear?" It was.

He went directly to the telephone. He didn't know exactly what he would say when the phone was answered. It didn't matter. It was just an I-know-Herculeah's-there-and-she'd-better-be-all-right call.

With trembling fingers he punched in the numbers. The line was not busy. It was ringing. He was expecting to hear the voice of the housekeeper, or Nurse Wegman, maybe even Herculeah herself. It was none of these.

"Pizza, pizza," a young male voice said. "Our special today is—"

"Sorry, wrong number," Meat said. He hung up the phone even though he was a little curious about the special. He dialed more carefully this time. The line was busy. He dialed several more times. Busy. He dialed the operator. He did not like to speak to operators, but this was an emergency.

"I've been dialing and dialing this number," Meat told her, "and I keep getting a busy signal. It's very important that I get through. A girl's life might depend upon it."

"I'll check the line."

Meat waited for an eternity.

"Sir?"

"Yes."

"That line appears to be out of order."

"Can you do something? Can you send somebody out there to fix it?"

"Probably not till Monday."

"But a girl's life might be at stake."

"I'll report it to customer service."

"But the girl is Herculeah," he told the operator as if that would make a difference. It should. "Herculeah's my best friend—actually she's pretty much my only real friend, but if Herculeah is your friend, you don't need any others."

"I'll tell customer service. Have a nice day."

And she was gone.

22

TERROR IN THE TOWER

Herculeah stood in front of the door that led to the tower. She listened. The house around her was quiet. The tower in front of her was quiet. Only the beating of her own heart broke the stillness.

The hallway was dark. There were no windows, and Herculeah wished for a flashlight. Or a candle. The book she had been reading to Mr. Hunt flashed into her mind. The girl in the book had also stood at the tower door. She had not had a flashlight or a candle. She had managed to proceed. So would Herculeah.

With one hand she felt for the keyhole. Her fingers found the opening, and her heart raced.

There was nothing like getting to the end of a mystery, Herculeah thought. Nothing like finding the last piece of the puzzle and setting it in place.

She took a deep breath, put the key in the lock, and turned. It resisted.

Another deep breath and a quick glance over her shoulder, and she turned the key the other way. With a click, the old lock yielded. Herculeah pulled the narrow, surprisingly heavy door toward her.

The hinges creaked loudly and Herculeah paused. She knew that anyone who was in the house would have heard that creak and known where she was.

As she waited to be discovered, she peered inside. The air that met her face was dank and cold. She could still turn back, she reminded herself, yet—just like the girl in the book—she could not. She stepped into the dark, unwelcoming interior of the tower.

She crossed the stone floor to the first of the circular stairs and looked up. Above her, the stairs twisted, snakelike, up the walls. They stopped at what appeared to be a trapdoor. Slowly Herculeah began to climb. She knew now that she had no control over the matter.

She continued up the stairs slowly, taking them one by one. Halfway up the stairs, she paused. She heard the sound of the tower door closing below her. Had it been a hand that closed it? She looked down. The thought that she might be trapped made her dizzy.

She touched the wall to steady herself. There was an eerie coldness to the stone beneath her hand.

She lifted her head. She listened.

She heard nothing, but she knew someone was up there, waiting for her.

And whoever it was knew she was coming. The creaking of the tower door would have given her away.

Slowly she took another step and another. Higher . . . higher. With each step, her fear grew until it seemed to swirl around her like a dark cape that held no warmth.

Herculeah continued to move slowly, deliberately up the stone stairs. Her steps were silent.

Suddenly she froze. She had heard a noise from the tower room above. She listened.

The noise was unlike anything she had heard before. It was not a human sound, nor was it the sound of an animal —at least no animal Herculeah had heard of.

It was breathing, and yet not ordinary breathing. It was a labored, troubling sound, almost a moan.

Herculeah glanced at one of the slotted windows. She could not see outside, but maybe the sound she had heard was the wind. A storm was coming. She knew that. She had seen the dark clouds. She had felt the rain. And now she could feel the wind moving around the tower.

What was it she had said to Mr. Hunt? "Dramatic things always happen during storms—though it's dramatic enough with something waiting for her at the top of the tower."

But, no, what she was hearing was not the wind around the tower. It was inside the tower.

Seven steps remained now.

It was just as it had been in the book, she thought, just as she had known it would be. But there would be no Meat waiting outside Hunt House to walk her home and make her laugh.

Six steps remained.

The trapdoor was overhead. Herculeah looked at it for a moment, trying to judge its weight. The wood was heavy. Perhaps it would take all her strength to open it.

She decided she would open it just a crack, just wide enough so she could see what was in the room. Then she could close it if she saw. . . . Her thoughts trailed off because she had no idea what she would see.

Five steps remained.

What was it she had said to Mr. Hunt? "People have climbed Everest in the time it's taken this girl to get to the top of the tower."

Four.

But then people want to get to the top of Everest.

Three.

She could go no higher without opening the trapdoor. She brushed her hands together, raised them, and, with all her strength, she pushed on the trapdoor.

Herculeah had misjudged. The trapdoor was not heavy at all.

Perhaps it was even on some sort of pulley, because the trapdoor sprang open.

Herculeah did not have time to see what awaited her in the tower room and to close the door if she didn't like what she saw.

The trapdoor seemed to pull her with it. Her momentum carried her into the tower room and left her sprawled across the dusty floor.

She lifted her head. She was not alone.

23

THE ANGEL OF DEATH

Meat walked slowly toward Haunt House. His mother had not wanted him to come here, but he had said, "I have to go, Mom, even though I may be in danger myself. I'm sorry if that causes you discomfort, but Herculeah needs me."

Well, actually, he had not said that. He had written it.

Well, actually he had not written those exact words. The note he had left pinned by a magnet to the refrigerator door said, "I've gone out—save me some pork chops."

The gate loomed ahead. He could make out the lions with their lifted claws.

He was still standing there, planning what he was going to do and say at the front door of Hunt House when he heard a car approach.

Meat closed his eyes. He knew it was his mother. It would be just like her. She treated him like a child! Probably as soon as she discovered he had left the house, she had grabbed her car keys.

He heard the window roll down. He waited for his mother's voice to say, "Albert Ambrose McMannis, you get in this car this minute." And he would get in the car like a good little boy—No, he would not!

He opened his eyes, turned and stared into the stony face of the Angel of Death herself—Nurse Wegman.

Meat had never particularly cared for nurses. They were mainly used, in Meat's experience, for carrying out orders too unpleasant for doctors to do themselves, like give shots.

Although Meat would rather it be Nurse Wegman than his mother, he still could not help noticing that Nurse Wegman was the kind of nurse who would carry out the most unpleasant orders with joy.

"What are you doing here?" Nurse Wegman asked.

"I tried to call, but   "

"I know. The phone's out."

Nurse Wegman waited, looking at him so fiercely that Meat wished car windows could be rolled up from the outside. If any engineer ever found himself being looked at by Nurse Wegman like that, he'd invent one.

"So what are you doing here?"

"I came about Herculeah."

"Who?"

"Herculeah, the girl who reads to Mr. Hunt."

"Oh, her." Nurse Wegman's look got even more unpleasant. "She's here?"

"I think so."

"In the house?"

"I think so."

"She couldn't be. There's nobody to let her in. I've fired the housekeeper."

"If Herculeah wanted to get in, she'd find a way."

Nurse Wegman's hands—they were big hands—hit the steering wheel in frustration. The horn, as if startled, gave a quick honk.

Nurse Wegman took a breath. "You go home. I had to leave to make a call . . . the . . . doctor. Mr. Hunt needs the doctor, and the doctor should be arriving any minute. The girl will have to be taken care of."

"Taken care of?" Meat asked. He didn't like the sound of that.

"She will have to—to go home."

"Oh."

"If she hasn't already gone, I mean."

"I guess she could've, though I didn't pass her on the way."

Nurse Wegman continued to stare at him. "Well, go on! Go!"

He continued to stand by the car. He couldn't leave. Herculeah was inside Hunt House—he knew that now—and she needed him.

As if reading his mind, Nurse Wegman said, "You aren't needed here."

Meat wished he could be sure of that.

"Go! Go!"

Still he could not move.

"May I give you some nursely advice?" Her tone was sweet now, but the same cold, bird-of-prey eyes watched him, as if swooping in for the kill.

"I guess."

"You need to lose some weight."

Meat drew in his breath. Nurse Wegman rolled up the window. Not until the car was halfway down the drive was Meat able to turn and take a few steps toward home.

When he was out of sight of the house, he stopped. He breathed deeply. He thought.

If I had not just thought about my dad . . . if I had not been reminded that my dad was my exact size at this age . . . if I had not been the son of Macho Man and a gentleman, I would have said, "And you, madam, need a shave."

But Son of Macho Man did not stoop to petty insults. He was a man of action.

Maybe he himself could not handle Nurse Wegman, but Son of Macho Man knew someone who could.

24

IN THE DEATH GRIP OF
A HUNDRED MEN

On the floor of the tower room, Herculeah lay where she had fallen, but only for a moment.

Then she scrambled to her feet. Her hands were fists. She was ready to do battle. What she saw caused her arms to sag. She took a step forward, moving away from the trapdoor.

Lying in front of her was a small woman. She lay on her side, curled toward Herculeah. Her face was streaked with blood and tears.

Around her lay—like remnants of an old picnic—crusts of bread, empty cups, a half-eaten apple, cake crumbs in an old napkin. Perhaps these offerings were what had been keeping the woman alive.

"Help me," the woman whispered. She reached out for Herculeah with a hand that trembled.

"What happened to you?"

"Help me."

"Yes, yes, of course I'll help you. Who are you?"

The woman spoke so softly Herculeah could not make out the words.

"Who?"

This time the words were clearer. "I'm Ida Wegman."

Herculeah took in a deep breath. "Wegman?"

"Yes."

"Nurse Wegman?"

"Yes. This man hit me on the head. . . ." Her eyes focused on Herculeah's for the first time. "It's coming back to me now. The man stopped me at the gate to ask directions, and before I knew what was happening, he struck me here." She raised her hand to the side of her head.

"Do you remember anything else?"

"He was a strong man. I remember he carried me up the circular stairs. He left me here . . . like this."

"Oh, my," Herculeah said. As she knelt beside the woman, her thoughts raced.

The man who hit her on the head is the man pretending to be Nurse Wegman. Nurse Wegman is a man! I should have known that. The first time we met him, he was dressed like a woman, but when he asked Meat a question, Meat answered, "Yes, sir." Sir! Meat sensed it, and I—like an idiot—

She broke off her thoughts.

"Listen, we've got to get out of here. The fake Nurse Wegman drove off in a car about an hour ago—I saw him leave—but he may come back, and we don't want to be up here in this tower if he does. We'd be trapped."

"Yes."

"Can you sit up?"

"If you help me."

Herculeah bent to put one arm around the woman's shoulder and raised her into a sitting position. The woman's head sagged against Herculeah.

"I'm dizzy."

"Take deep breaths," Herculeah advised. "Can you stand?"

"I don't think so."

"Then I'd better go for help."

"No, no, don't leave me. I'll stand. Just don't let go of me."

Herculeah lifted the woman into a standing position, but her legs crumpled and she sank back to the floor.

"I'll go for help."

"You won't come back."

"I will."

"Someone went for help before."

"Who?" Herculeah's thoughts lifted with the hope that help might already be on the way.

"An old woman. Very old. She brought me food. I asked her to call the police. She said Papa wouldn't like it."

"Oh." Herculeah realized that she meant Miss Hunt. She realized, too, that Miss Hunt's way of helping was by throwing a blood-stained coat out of the tower, by leaving phone messages, by opening the front door to let Herculeah inside, by leaving the key to the tower where she would find it. The old woman was like a child. She wouldn't call the police because Papa wouldn't like it.

"I've got to go for help."

"Don't leave me."

The woman's arms encircled Herculeah's legs with surprising strength. Her face was pressed against Herculeah's knees. Herculeah tried to move her legs, but she couldn't even take a step.

"If I don't go for help, we might—" She didn't want to say the word "die." That would upset the woman even more. "We might be trapped here."

The woman lifted her head. "Was that a car?"

"You heard a car?"

"I don't know. I heard something."

"Maybe it was the storm. I hope that's what it was, but I've got to get out of here. You have to let go of my legs."

"No! No! You'll leave me!" she wailed.

Herculeah pulled at the woman's arms, but her grip was like steel.

Herculeah had heard of something like this. It was called a

death grip. It happened when people who were dying suddenly got enormous strength and could hold on to someone so tightly a hundred men couldn't break the grip.

Herculeah didn't think the woman was dying, but she did think she had a death grip a hundred men couldn't break.

"Look," Herculeah said in her most reasonable and, she hoped, reassuring voice, "at least loosen your grip a little, just enough so that I can get over to the trapdoor and close it."

"No, it's a trick. As soon as you get over there you'll go down the stairs and leave. I won't be left again. I won't. I'll die if I'm left again."

"Look, let's inch over to the trapdoor. You can be with me every step of the way. We'll go over slowly. I'll close the door and we'll sit on it. That way, if the man does come back, he won't be able to get up here, and sooner or later my mom will come to see what's wrong and—"

She didn't finish because at that moment she heard something that froze her blood.

She heard the creaking of the tower door as it opened. Then she heard a heavy footstep on the stairs.

It's too late, she told herself, he's here.

A MURDERER'S CHILD

Herculeah lunged toward the trapdoor. She was determined to get there even if she had to crawl, dragging this wounded woman with her. The woman screamed with pain as they fell to the floor, but she did not loosen her grip.

The footsteps on the circular stairs were coming closer. Herculeah was on her stomach now, pulling herself along with her elbows, but the woman was a terrible burden. She reached for the trapdoor, but there was not enough time.

A huge hand reached in the opening, holding the trapdoor in place, and Nurse Wegman's—the wrong Nurse Wegman's—face appeared in the opening. Then his chest. With his weight on his arms, he pulled himself up and sat in the opening, his feet swinging down over the circular stairs. The look on his face told Herculeah he was enjoying himself.

The woman moaned. Herculeah felt her arms go limp. She had fainted, and now—too late—Herculeah was free.

"It's you," she said. She got to her feet and began to move away from the trapdoor.

"You should have stayed away," the man said. "This was no concern of yours."

"I guess I made it my concern."

"That was a mistake."

"You're no nurse."

"Never have been."

"No woman."

Another cruel smile. "Never have been."

"You're one of the Hunt family, though, aren't you?"

"Lionus Hunt the Second, at your service."

"I thought so. You've got the Hunt eyes." Herculeah did not intend that as a compliment.

Herculeah took another step back. The man stood and glanced down at the unconscious woman at his feet. Herculeah thought he was going to step over her body and come after her, but he did not.

Herculeah said, "Does all this"—she made a gesture that took in his disguise, the woman's body, the whole house—"have to do with that family reunion?"

"That was a long time ago. How did you find out about that?"

"I read about it in a news clipping." Herculeah kept talking. She knew from past experience that when you were facing a killer, you kept talking. "There was a game at the reunion— hide-and-seek, I believe."

"Yes, a child's game."

"The governess was killed. A stone was thrown from this tower, I believe."

"The stone wasn't meant for the governess."

"Who then?"

"My mother's twin sister."

"And who threw the stone?"

"My mother."

Herculeah said, "Your mother hated her own twin that much—enough to try to kill her?"

"Oh, yes. Her twin was the good one. Everyone loved her twin. It started as jealousy, I guess—normal in sisters. It was petty things at first. She'd hide her twin's toys, spill her milk, make her cry."

He paused, and Herculeah said quickly, "But it didn't stop there."

"No, it got physical. She would shove her twin, push her down the stairs. Once she even stabbed her twin's portrait with a knife."

"That should have been a warning to the family."

"Oh, my mother was punished all right, but that only made her hate her twin more."

"What happened then?"

"There were several accidents—near misses, like the stone from the tower. I believe it was the poison mushrooms that finally did her in."

"Your mother gave her poison mushrooms?"

"The family thought so. They kicked her out. She was only seventeen." He glanced down at the unconscious woman at his feet before he continued. "But my mother is dying now, half out of her mind with pain. I just went out to call her for more instructions and only got babbling. Earlier I managed to piece the story together. I didn't even know she had a twin. She had never even mentioned her family. Now I learn that not only is there a family, but a family with a great deal of money. And this money is quite probably hidden in the family house."

"And you had to get inside."

"Yes."

"But you're family. Why couldn't you just come for a visit?"

"The family made my mother an offer she couldn't refuse. They wouldn't contact the police if she would leave. The old man didn't trust the police, but he mistrusted her even more. She left, and I—a murderer's child—would not have been welcome." He gave that cruel smile that Herculeah was beginning to hate. "Because a murderer's child could also turn out to be a murderer, don't you think?"

"But you haven't murdered anybody. The nurse is still alive."

"I just wanted her out of the way. So you're right. I haven't killed anyone. Not yet." Another smile, and then he changed the subject. "Once I came here and saw the situation, it wasn't hard to make plans. It was simple. I'd take the place of one of the nurses. I'd find the money. I'd leave with nobody the wiser."

"But how did you get the nurse up here? I almost got lost just finding the tower door."

"I slipped in the house through the side door. So convenient. The door led directly into the hall and the tower door. My mother told me a lot of shortcuts. She knew how to get around in the house without being noticed."

"The tower door was locked, wasn't it?"

"Anybody could open these old locks, if"—he touched his pocket—"if he had the right knife."

Herculeah drew in her breath. He had a knife! To divert him, she said quickly, "You haven't found the money! There may not even be any money."

"I think there is. All I have to do . . ." He trailed off.

Herculeah could sense a subtle change in him. His body was no longer relaxed; he was ready in a way he had not been before.

"Listen," she said, stepping back, "my friend knows I'm here. He'll tell my father. My father's a police detective."

"I've taken care of your friend."

"What? You did something to Meat? What?"

Now Herculeah was also ready in a way she had not been before.

"If you hurt Meat . . ."

She stepped forward, prepared for battle. Now the unconscious body of the woman was all that lay between them.

The woman stirred. She lifted her head. It came to her that

just before she lost consciousness, she had held on to legs. Those legs had been all that lay between her and death.

With a cry, she reached out for the only legs she saw—the wrong Nurse Wegman's.

"What?" he cried. "What are you doing? Get off, you fool."

He took a step back, trying to escape the clutching hands, but his heel caught in the opening of the trapdoor.

"Push!" Herculeah cried.

She waited with her heart in her throat to see if the woman had the strength to obey.

26

SON OF MACHO MAN

Meat rubbed his hands over his sweatshirt to dry them of sweat. He tried to calm himself by humming "Macho Man." When his hands were as dry as they were going to get, he turned to the pay phone. He deposited the coins in the slot, dialed the number, and waited for three rings.

A voice said, "Police Department. Zone three. This is Sergeant Rossini. Can I help you?"

Meat cleared his throat. "I sure hope so," he said. "I need to speak to Detective Chico Jones. It's important."

"What's the problem?"

"It's about his daughter. She's—"

"Herculeah?"

Meat sighed with relief. Everyone in the county—in the United States, probably—knew Herculeah. "Yes, sir. There's something he needs to know. Herculeah may be in trouble."

"Is this, er, some kind of personal problem? I've met Mrs.

Jones, Herculeah's mom, and she seems to be the kind of woman who can handle most anything."

"I can't get her—just her answering machine—and I believe this is a matter for the police. Also, I'm at a pay phone and I'm running out of coins."

"I'll see if he's in." There was a pause.

Meat waited. When the police put you on hold, they didn't bother piping in soothing music to ease the wait. You just had to hold the phone and hope for the best.

Since there was nothing else to do, Meat let his thoughts continue. The chorus of "Macho Man" would have been a perfect waiting song for him.

Other callers, of course, might like something different, something to lift their spirits. What was the name of that song that went, "When you walk through a storm, hold your head up," or something like that? A lady sang it in an old movie.

Anybody calling the police was bound to be in some kind of storm. That was a given. You wouldn't want to walk through them with your head up, however, because—

"Chico Jones," a voice said.

"Oh, hi." Meat was brought back from his musical interlude abruptly. "Thank you for taking the call, Mr. Jones. It's me from across the street."

"Albert?"

"Yes."

"What's up?"

"Herculeah's at a place called Hunt House, and I think she may be in trouble."

"I spoke with her mom this morning, and she assured me Herculeah wasn't going back there anymore to read to Mr. Hunt."

"I don't think she went there to read."

"I'll check into it. Where are you?"

"I'm at a gas station. It's not far from the house. I could meet you at the gate to Hunt House, if you don't mind. I'm worried."

"I'm on my way. See you there."

Meat hung up the phone.

A customer had heard Meat's side of the conversation and gotten interested. She said, "Is everything all right?"

"I hope so," Meat said, then added what was causing him to continue sweating, "if we're not too late."

27

ON THE TOWER STAIRS

"Push!" Herculeah shouted again.

The woman did not seem to hear her. She seemed intent on only one thing—not being left alone in the tower again.

"Help me! Help!" She was pleading with the man now. "Please!" He was no longer the man who had wounded her; he was her salvation.

"Let go of me, you fool!"

She managed to get to her knees, but she had no intention of letting go. The struggle to her knees was too much. She fell forward, and as she fell forward, the man fell backward.

Herculeah gasped. She saw what was going to happen. The man was going to fall down the tower stairs, and his momentum would take the woman with him.

Herculeah rushed forward. In two strides she was there. She encircled the woman's body with her arms.

For one terrible moment the three of them were locked together at the top of the stairs.

"Push!" Herculeah cried, and this time, the woman had a moment of clarity. She understood. This was the man who had hurt her. This was the man who wanted to kill her. This was the man they were trying to get away from. She pushed.

The three of them fell at the same time. Herculeah fell backward. She sat down hard on the tower floor. The woman fell with her, landing on Herculeah's lap like a child.

The man teetered for a moment on the edge of the stone steps. Then, with a terrible scream, he went over the edge, hitting his head hard on the edge of the trapdoor as he disappeared.

The nurse moaned. "What happened?"

"You saved our lives. That's what happened."

Herculeah lost no time. She shifted the woman's body to the floor and got to her feet. She moved quickly to the opening of the trapdoor and peered down the stairs. She was prepared to slam the trapdoor shut if the man was conscious and likely to come up to the tower room again.

She didn't think he was going anywhere. He lay halfway down the stairs. He was not moving. His eyes stared blindly up at her.

As she looked at his thick features, the shadow of stubble on his face, she wondered how she had ever mistaken him for a woman.

121

"He was the man at the gate, the man who hit me," the woman said, speaking as if she was trying to get the facts straight in her mind.

"Oh, yes," said Herculeah.

"He would have killed us."

"That, too," Herculeah said.

"Is he gone now?"

"Yes. He's on the stairs. He's unconscious, though, so he won't be bothering us anymore. I'm going for help."

She kept her distance because she was afraid the woman might try again to restrain her, but the woman seemed to be lucid now. Herculeah went down one step without incident.

"Will you see the old woman who tried to help me?"

"I don't know. Miss Hunt comes and goes. She did try to help you, but in her own way. She couldn't call the police. . . ."

"Papa wouldn't have liked it," the woman said with a faint smile.

Herculeah smiled back. "Exactly. But she did the best she could. Did you know she threw your coat from the tower to let us know you were here?"

"I remember her calling to someone, 'She's up here, up here,' but nobody came."

"Finally, I got the message and I came. Now I do have to go. You need a doctor. That man needs a doctor, and Mr. Hunt does, too. You'll be fine now."

The sound of the woman's voice followed Herculeah down three more steps, though Herculeah couldn't make out her words. She knew the woman was remembering more and more of her ordeal.

Halfway down the stairs lay the man's body. It blocked Herculeah's way. The stairs were narrow. There was no room between his body and the stone wall, but there was a small space to the outside of the steps. She would have to be very careful.

She paused for a moment, examining the man. He had not moved. His eyes were blank. But he was breathing. He was still alive.

She took one more step, then one more. The man's shoulders were broad and blocked the next two stairs. She would have to step over him, but then the danger would be over. She could fly down the rest of the steps and be on her way.

Just this one long step.

She took a deep breath. She was lifting her foot when the man's eyes focused. She did not see this, but she knew something had happened by a sudden twitch in his shoulder muscle. She must move quickly.

At that exact moment, she felt his fingers encircle her other foot. Not another death grip! she screamed to herself. Then she let out a real scream. It echoed within the circular walls, and seemed to go on and on.

"Let me go!"

Then from the bottom of the stairs came an old quavering voice. "Let her go or I'll shoot."

Both Herculeah and the man looked down the stairs. At the bottom, gun in hand, stood old Miss Hunt. In her trembling hands was a gun.

AT GUNPOINT

This was the oldest gun Herculeah had ever seen in her life. This gun would probably have been outdated in the Civil War.

Herculeah knew instantly that she was in much more danger from Miss Hunt with a gun than she was from the man lying beside her. Already his hand was losing its grip on her ankle.

"Don't shoot, Miss Hunt," Herculeah said.

"Wants to kill us."

"Put the gun down. We're fine."

"I'll kill him first."

"Miss Hunt—"

"His mother killed my sister."

"Maybe she did or maybe it was an accident."

"No accident." The gun was waving back and forth, and Miss Hunt held it with both hands to steady it. One finger was on the trigger.

"He's sly."

"Yes," Herculeah agreed.

"He pretended to be a nurse. Didn't fool me."

"No." Herculeah's ankle was free now, and she went down one step. "He's hurt now. He can't harm us."

"Pretending to be hurt."

"He's not pretending. He's unconscious. Look at him." Herculeah reached down and touched his shoulder. "See? Now put the gun down."

Herculeah straightened. She came down the rest of the stairs slowly. Her hands were raised in the classic gesture of having no weapon.

She paused at the bottom of the stairs. Miss Hunt backed away from the tower, through the open door, and into the hallway beyond. The gun was still pointed in Herculeah's direction.

"Please put the gun down. I have so much I want to tell you, but I can't tell you with that gun pointed at me."

"This is an old gun. Won't hurt anyone."

"I'm afraid of *all* guns," Herculeah said truthfully.

"This was Papa's gun. It's never been shot. It's not even loaded."

She pointed the gun upward, pulled the trigger, and blew a hole in the ceiling.

"Well, I'll be," she said.

There was a moment of silence while the smoke cleared, and then a voice broke the silence. "I'll take that gun."

It was the voice of a man, a man of authority.

Herculeah had covered her ears with her hands when the gun went off. She lowered her hands now and saw Meat.

She couldn't believe that Meat had spoken in such a manly way. She had always thought he had the same aversion to guns as she did.

Then she looked behind Meat and saw her father.

Miss Hunt was eyeing her father's outstretched hand with suspicion. She looked at his face. "Are you the police?" she asked.

"I am."

"Papa never wanted the police here."

"But your papa would have wanted you to give me the gun." Her father's voice was kind, reassuring, forceful.

"Here," Miss Hunt said. She thrust the gun on him. Then in a moment she disappeared down the hall with only a wisp of smoke from the old gun to show she had ever been there.

Her father handed the gun to an officer behind him.

"You'll never, never know how glad I am to see you!" Herculeah cried. She opened her arms and rushed forward.

Meat thought for one glorious moment she was coming to throw her arms around him. He was just getting his hands out of his jacket pockets so he could participate in the hug when she rushed past him and threw her arms around her father.

"Dad! Dad! How did you know I was in trouble? How did you know to come?"

"You can thank your friend for that. Albert called me. Then I got your mom on her cell phone. She's been worried about you—obviously with good reason. You're all right?"

"Yes, now that you're here I'm fine."

"Let's go where we can talk."

"There's a man on the stairs." She nodded toward the stairs behind her without leaving the safety of her dad's arms. "And up in the tower room there's the real Nurse Wegman. She has a head injury, and . . . oh, it was too much for me." She buried her head in her father's chest.

"It's not your problem anymore. I'll get some officers to see about them. I've got half the police force here with me."

She lifted her head. "And old Mr. Hunt—the man I was reading to upstairs—was unconscious when I left him."

"Check upstairs, too," he told an officer.

Herculeah glanced over her shoulder and saw Meat. "And Meat!" she said, acknowledging him at last. "How did you get here?"

"I was waiting out by the gate, and your dad gave me a lift the rest of the way." He did not mention that the only good way to arrive at Haunt House was in a police car with two policemen in the front seat.

"Meat filled me in on some of what happened, but you'll have to tell me the rest."

They walked down the hall, and Herculeah was gracious enough to call over her shoulder, "You come, too, Meat. I need you."

He came.

29

OH, MOM

"I see now that I absolutely cannot trust you," Herculeah's mother said.

Herculeah said, "Oh, Mom."

"You're worse than an infant. I ought to have my head examined for asking you to read to Mr. Hunt. I should have known you'd go poking your nose in where it didn't belong."

Herculeah and her mom were driving home through the black gates of Hunt House. They were in the front seat of the car, talking. Meat sat alone in the backseat, listening.

They had seen the two Nurse Wegmans and Mr. Hunt loaded into ambulances and on their way to the hospital. They had waited for the housekeeper to arrive and look after the sister. "I knew something was wrong about that nurse as soon as she fired me," the housekeeper had said. Now the three of them were on their way home.

Herculeah glanced at her mom's profile. Sometimes her mom really looked like a private detective.

"If you'd tell me things, then I wouldn't have to poke my nose in, as you put it. Well, can I ask you one thing?"

"You can ask."

"You were hired to find the sister, right? And you had located her when all this happened?"

"I had located her address. The lawyer was going to contact her."

"Why did they need the sister? They kicked her out a long time ago. For the mushrooms."

"Mushrooms?"

"The poison ones. It's a long story, Mom."

"They did kick her out, but they need her now. They want to sell the house—there's going to be a mall there—and they can't sell without consent of all parties. The sister is one of the parties."

"So what's going to happen to the nurses?"

"There's only one real nurse."

"I know that."

Her mother sighed. "Your dad thinks that neither of them has injuries that are life-threatening, although the man who impersonated a nurse is going to face serious charges—attempted murder for one. And it was all for nothing."

"Why do you say that?"

"He came to Hunt House thinking there was money hidden

in the house, when the only thing of value is the property itself. He and his mother would have gotten a third of that."

Herculeah glanced out the window to see if she could get a final glimpse of Hunt House. Only the tip of the tower rose above the trees. "I guess I'll never come back to Hunt House."

"Why would you want to?"

"The book, Mom! To finish the book. I know what I found at the top of the tower, but I don't know what the girl in the book found."

"Maybe I can get the book for you, but if you go to the hospital to read to Mr. Hunt, I suggest you take another book."

"Of course, Mom."

Meat spoke from the backseat. "Tell your mom what your dad said about the end of the book."

Herculeah glanced around as if surprised to see him there. It had been so long since anyone noticed him that he was surprised to find himself there. "I was just getting ready to," she said.

She turned back to her mom. "I was puzzled about why Mr. Hunt chose the book. I mean, maybe he read it as a child, or maybe he wanted me to see the clipping, or maybe he sensed danger in the tower. I said I was mainly curious about the end of the book and what was up in the tower, and he said, 'Oh, I can tell you what was at the top of the tower if that's all you want to know—Batman.'"

Herculeah laughed. "I thought he meant like Batman and

Robin, but he meant 'Batman' like Dracula. He admitted he hadn't read the book, of course, but he claimed to have seen the movie. It was very funny. I wish I could imitate him so—"

"Don't bother."

There was silence, broken only by an uneasy cough from the backseat. Meat felt that the front seat could take a lesson from him. When you were about to say something wrong, cough.

Herculeah's mom didn't believe in coughs. She said, "Your dad picked an inappropriate time to be amusing."

"Mom, you don't understand Dad at all!"

"Oh?"

"It was the perfect time. I was upset and it helped me. At least he didn't say I was worse than an infant. You know what he said?"

"No."

"He said that whatever the girl in the book found in the tower, she couldn't possibly have handled it any better than I did."

In the backseat, Meat waited for Mrs. Jones's reply, but apparently she had used up all of her one-word sentences. They drove the rest of the way home in a blessed silence.

30

A MIDNIGHT CALLER

The phone rang and Herculeah picked it up on the first ring. She said, "Hi, Meat."

"How did you know it was me? Has your mom gotten caller ID?"

"I don't need caller ID to know when it's you. And," she went on, "you always call when we've solved a case."

"I didn't do much to solve this one."

"Yes, you did. You recognized right away that Nurse Wegman was a man. And I didn't pick up on that at all. I was an idiot. I thought she was just an unattractive woman. Sometimes I think I don't deserve to be a detective."

"Oh, yes, you do. You manage to get people to confess things, like Lionus Hunt telling you all about his mother killing her twin sister, about his plans to get into Hunt House in the disguise of a nurse. He would have thought it was a waste of time to tell me stuff like that. He would have just killed me."

"If I've learned one thing about criminals, it's that they think they're so clever, they want to talk about how they did it."

There was a silence, and then Herculeah said, "You know what I was thinking about when you called?"

"What?"

"I was thinking about the connection between this case and the labors of the real Hercules."

"It had to be the Nemean lion. Remember Hercules killed him? There were wrought-iron lions on the gate? Did you notice them? And the old man's name was Lionus."

"Yes, I noticed the lions. I saw them the first day I went to read."

"Did your hair frizzle?"

"No, but I got a this-is-it feeling. When I get that feeling—it's hard to describe. I just know . . ." She took a deep breath, searching for the right words. "I just know . . ."

"This is it," Meat supplied.

"Exactly!" She hesitated. "Why are you laughing at my feeling?"

"I'm not laughing at that. I just thought of another Hercules connection."

"What?"

"Remember the girdle of Hippo-something? I forget what her name was."

"Hippolyte. But I don't get what that's got to do with it."

"The girdle. The imposter Nurse Wegman wore one to help

him look like a woman. I saw it when they were putting him in the ambulance."

Herculeah laughed, too.

Meat waited and then got to the real reason he had called. "You haven't asked me about the phone call from my dad."

"Meat! I'm sorry! I can't believe I forgot. How was the phone call from your dad?"

"It was great. He's going to be here next weekend."

"I hope I get to see him. I only saw him that one night, and he was dressed like Macho Man."

"He even looks like Macho Man in his everyday clothes, too."

"So what are you and your dad going to do? Anything special?"

Meat hesitated, trying to decide whether to say, "Oh, nothing special, just hang out," or tell the truth. He decided on the truth. "My dad has this friend who runs a health club here. My dad trained there when he was getting started. He's getting me a membership, and I'm going there every weekend."

"Lucky! I wish my dad would get me a membership. What's the name of it?"

"I forgot," he said. Meat didn't want to seem unfriendly, but he did hope that he and Herculeah would not be in training together. This was something between two Macho Men.

To change the subject he said, "Have you got any idea yet about what your next mystery will be?"

"I not only have an idea, I know."

"How?"

"Well, when I was searching Ida Wegman's coat, I reached in the pocket and pulled out a lipstick. It was Summer Rose or something like that. And I knew it wasn't the fake Nurse Wegman's lipstick because she'd wear something like Dragon-Lady Red. And as soon as I thought, Dragon, I knew that would be part of my next case."

"One of those this-is-it feelings?"

"Yes."

Meat said, "Dragon . . . dragon. . . . There are no live dragons, of course. Maybe this has something to do with that Chinese martial arts place or that Chinese restaurant on Peachtree. Both of them have dragons in their windows."

"No. This will not be a dragon advertisement. This will be a dragon."

She yawned. Meat always dreaded that sound because it meant the conversation was over. He tried to think of some way to keep it going, but before he could, she spoke again.

"I've got to go. It's been a long day. I'll see you tomorrow. Good night, Meat."

There were only three words left to say, so he said them.

"Good night, Herculeah."